The Chronos Resurgence

Echoes of Time

James "JimDandy" Dennis

Dedication

This piece of work is dedicated to all those brave souls who served in the US Military and those Combat Veterans who fought for our freedom. It is in memory of those who sacrificed everything they had for the love of their country.

Acknowledgment

I would like to acknowledge a few very important people in my life who have always been there for me. First of all, I would like to thank my wife, Christine Dennis, and Family for always supporting me in all my endeavors.

A very special thanks to Dan Brown Academy for their great services.

About the Author

James "JimDandy" Dennis was born in Fairfield, California. He attained a Bachelor's degree in Social Sciences from Troy University. He served for 20 years in the US Army as an infantryman and showed his skills as an Airborne Ranger when sent on combat tours in Panama, Africa, and Afghanistan.

James Dennis continued to support the Army by working as a contractor, where he made more trips to Afghanistan to support the troops with surveillance and other technical systems. He is now a member of the Combat Veterans Motorcycle Association® Chapter 15-1 in North Carolina, an association of Veterans helping Veterans.

He is passionate about writing and has a strong desire to pen down the stories of his dreams and imaginations in a book.

Preface

In the year 2360, Ethan discovers the Chronos Resurgence, an enigmatic device with the ability to transform the universe, and his life in the technological utopia of Prime Meridian takes a thrilling turn. Ethan starts to reveal the mysteries of this mysterious device thanks to his irrational curiosity and aptitude for tinkering with artifacts and relics.

Ethan meets a fascinating variety of people as he digs deeper into the Chronos Resurgence; each character brings excitement and realism to his adventure. Among them, Zin Xia, a captivating personality with a mysterious goal, plays a crucial role in his quest.

Every discovery and experiment becomes a heart-pounding journey into the uncharted, where science fiction and reality converge. With the Chronos Resurgence's power at his disposal, Ethan faces a future rife with unfathomable possibilities - and unpredictable repercussions.

Ethan's seemingly routine life becomes a fantastic voyage in this gripping story of discovery and invention. Even as uncertainty looms, hope propels him forward. Ethan is prepared to seize the future, one risky discovery at a time, as the world of 2360 teeters on the verge of change.

The story told in "Chronos Resurgence: Echoes of Time" is one of adventure, love, unity, and the profound mysteries of time.

Contents

Dedication... i

Acknowledgment.. ii

About the Author.. iii

Preface... iv

Prologue: Threads Of Destiny 1

Chapter 1: The Chronos Resurgence 10

Chapter 2: The Future Within the Past........................... 17

Chapter 3: Temporal Defense Corps.............................. 24

Chapter 4: Zin Xia.. 32

Chapter 5: Echoes of Ancient China 39

Chapter 6: Threads Of Destiney..................................... 46

Chapter 7: To Where Time Takes Us 53

Chapter 8: Looping Through the Timeline...................... 61

Chapter 9: Temporal Symphony in Zrerphis.................. 69

Chapter 10: Unraveling Threads..................................... 81

Chapter 11: Echoes of Destiny....................................... 88

Chapter 12: Threads Intertwined 97

Chapter 13: Weaver's Web.. 105

Chapter 14: Desperate Gambit....................................... 113

Chapter 15: The Nexus Point 122

Chapter 16: Love's Resilience 131

Chapter 17: The Paradox 140

Chapter 18: A Journey Beyond Time 149

Chapter 19: Building a Legacy.. 159

Chapter 20: Eternity's Embrace 169

Epilogue: Threads of Eternity 176

Prologue: Threads Of Destiny

In the year 2360, the world stands as a testament to human innovation and technological achievement. It's a time when the scientific boundaries of what was once considered impossible have been shattered. This era is marked by several key developments that have reshaped every aspect of human existence from the very nature of society itself. Humanity has perfected the art of clean and virtually limitless energy generation. Solar panels, fusion reactors, and advanced geothermal systems provide power in abundance. This energy revolution has not only solved the climate crisis but also eliminated concerns about resource scarcity. It powers homes, industries, and even interstellar spacecraft with ease.

Transportation has undergone a transformative evolution. Personal flying vehicles, powered by silent and efficient electric propulsion systems, are a common sight in cities. Maglev trains move at speeds unimaginable in the past, connecting continents within hours. And for those who wish to explore the cosmos, commercial space travel has become accessible, with regular flights to the Moon and Mars.

Medicine has also seen remarkable advances. The concept of aging, as we once knew it, has been redefined. With the advent of advanced genetic therapies and nanotechnology, humans can now live well beyond a century in peak physical and mental health. Common diseases have been eradicated, and even previously untreatable conditions are now curable. Medical diagnoses are made with pinpoint accuracy through the use of nanobots that continuously monitor health, and treatments are tailored to our individual genetic makeup.

Artificial intelligence has evolved to become an integral part of daily life. Personal AI assistants manage your schedule, understand your emotions, and offer emotional support when needed. They have become companions, helping people navigate the complexities of an interconnected world. AI-driven systems have also revolutionized industries like finance, agriculture, and manufacturing, making them more efficient and sustainable. The world of work has seen a radical transformation. Automation and AI have taken over many routine tasks, allowing humans to focus on creative, meaningful work. The concept of a universal basic income has been implemented in many countries, providing economic security to all citizens and enabling them to pursue their passions and interests.

Society itself has undergone significant changes. With advances in communication technology, language barriers have largely disappeared. People can communicate effortlessly in any language, fostering a global sense of unity. Cultural exchange and understanding have reached unprecedented levels, leading to more rapid information exchange. Environmental conservation is at the forefront of global priorities. The world has shifted to a circular economy, where waste is minimized and resources are reused and recycled. Education has become a lifelong journey, with learning opportunities available to people of all ages and backgrounds. Virtual reality and augmented reality technologies have revolutionized the way we learn.

Prime Meridian, a bustling metropolis situated at the heart of a vast and diverse landscape, stands as stark proof of human ingenuity and ambition. With its skyline stretching toward extraordinary heights and its streets alive with the constant hum of activity, this city embodies the very essence of progress and innovation. At the core of Prime Meridian lies a thriving urban center characterized by its towering skyscrapers, their glass facades reflecting the ever-changing sky. The cityscape is a mesmerizing blend of modern architectural wonders and timeless classics, a juxtaposition of sleek, contemporary designs and historic landmarks that stand as a nod to the city's rich past. The streets of Prime Meridian foster people from all walks of life to converge here, creating a diverse and dynamic community. Bustling marketplaces offer an array of goods from around the world, and each vendor's stall is a microcosm of global commerce. The aromas of street food waft through the air, tantalizing the senses with flavors from every corner of the globe.

Transportation in Prime Meridian is a marvel of efficiency. An intricate network of renewably powered subways, buses, and trams crisscrosses the city, ensuring that residents and visitors can easily navigate its sprawling expanse. The central business district located in the center of Prime Meridian is a bustling hub of economic activity that truly reflects the spirit of growth and progress. High-rise buildings house the headquarters of multinational corporations, financial institutions, and startups alike. The city's stock exchange buzzes with activity, a hub of global commerce where fortunes are made and lost with the click of a button. Entrepreneurs flock here, drawn by the promise of innovation and opportunity.

Education is a cornerstone of Prime Meridian's success. Its universities and research institutions are renowned worldwide, attracting scholars and students from every corner of the globe. The pursuit of knowledge is not confined to academia; it permeates every aspect of life in the city. Museums, galleries, and libraries abound, celebrating the arts, sciences, and humanities. Green spaces provide respite from the urban hustle and bustle. Parks, gardens, and plazas are meticulously landscaped, offering tranquil oases amidst the city's relentless energy. Families gather in these serene settings, children playing in the shadow of skyscrapers while adults find solace in the natural beauty that coexists with modernity. Innovation pulses through the veins of Prime Meridian. Tech startups thrive in co-working spaces and incubators, fostering an environment of collaboration and creativity.

Culture thrives in Prime Meridian, where theaters, concert halls, and art galleries offer a myriad of experiences. The city's diverse population ensures that cultural celebrations and festivals are a constant fixture, each one a vibrant reminder of the city's global heritage.

* * *

Ethan, on the surface, appeared to be an ordinary guy. He lived in a cozy apartment in a quiet neighborhood of Prime Meridian. His daily life was defined by routines and responsibilities that mirrored those of countless others in the busy city. However, beneath this façade of normalcy lay an absorbing passion for exploration and an uncanny talent for tinkering with relics and artifacts that had captivated his imagination since childhood.

Each day, Ethan's alarm clock chimed precisely at 6:30 a.m. He'd roll out of bed, never needing a second alarm or to 'snooze' the first one. After a quick breakfast, Ethan would don his neatly pressed suit and tie, ready to face the challenges of the workday. He worked as a project manager at one of Prime Meridian's leading technology firms. His job involved coordinating teams, meeting deadlines, and navigating the intricacies of corporate culture. It was a demanding role that required precision and attention to detail, qualities that he had honed over the years of dedication.

As Ethan walked to the nearby hovercraft station, he blended in seamlessly with the crowd of commuters. Each person is lost in their own thoughts and daily concerns. But hidden beneath the surface, a burning desire for exploration and discovery smoldered within him. It was a passion that had taken root in his early years, nurtured by countless hours spent reading science fiction novels and watching space exploration go from documentaries to real life in front of his eyes. At lunchtime, Ethan would often slip away from the office, finding solace in a nearby park. He'd sit on a bench, a sandwich in hand, and lose himself in the pages of a well-worn exploration journal. In those moments, he was transported to distant galaxies and unexplored worlds he believed he would one day see for himself.

Ethan's colleagues often regarded him as a man of routines, unaware of the treasure trove of relics and artifacts hidden in the depths of his apartment. For Ethan, these items were more than mere curiosities; they were windows into the world. Ethan's apartment was physical evidence of his passion—a comfortable space filled with an eclectic mix of vintage technology and memorabilia. An old astronaut helmet sat on a display stand in one corner of the living room. It was a genuine artifact from the early days of space travel, a relic that had once protected an astronaut as they ventured into the vacuum of space. Ethan had painstakingly restored the helmet, taking him the better part of a month. His most prized possession, however, was a piece of a meteorite that had fallen to Earth centuries ago. It had traveled countless miles through the cosmos before landing on our planet, a fragment of a distant world.

Evenings in Ethan's apartment were a blend of routines and indulgence in his passion for relics. After a long day at the office, he would change into more comfortable attire and make a cup of tea. The soft glow of vintage space-themed lamps bathed his living room in a warm, inviting light as he engrossed himself in his favorite pastime.

Ethan's workbench was a focal point of his apartment. It held an assortment of tools, each meticulously organized, and a magnifying glass for delicate repairs. It was here that he poured his heart and soul into restoring artifacts to their former glory. Whether it was a vintage space helmet, a mechanical calculator from a bygone era, or a historic piece of technology, Ethan approached each restoration with the precision and care of an artist. One of his ongoing projects was a vintage astrolabe, a celestial navigation instrument from centuries past. Its gears had long been frozen in place; its brass surface tarnished with time. But to Ethan, it was a puzzle waiting to be solved. He would spend hours delicately cleaning each gear, applying just the right amount of oil to ensure it moved smoothly once more. As he worked, he would imagine ancient mariners using similar instruments to navigate the vast oceans, guided by the stars.

As the night wore on, Ethan's apartment would come alive with the soft hum of his workbench lamp and the occasional clink of tools against metal. In these quiet moments, he felt most connected to his passion, as if he were on a solitary voyage through time and space.

Ethan's weekends were dedicated to exploring the relics and artifacts of Prime Meridian itself. He would often visit antique shops, flea markets, and auctions, always on the lookout for hidden gems that held a piece of history. Whether it was an old tram ticket from the early days of public transportation or a vintage typewriter that had once belonged to a renowned author, Ethan was eager to grow his collection. He also had a penchant for documenting his discoveries. His apartment held a collection of journals filled with sketches, notes, and stories inspired by the relics he encountered. Each artifact told a tale of the people who had created it, used it, and left their mark in time.

Ethan's collection of relics and artifacts often raised eyebrows among his friends and family, who found his eccentricities both charming and amusing. One evening, as he gathered with his closest friends in his apartment, the topic of his quirky collection couldn't be avoided. Jessica, his childhood friend, sipped her tea and peered curiously at an odd contraption on his shelf. It resembled a cross between a bicycle and a pogo stick, with an intricate arrangement of pedals and springs.

"Ethan, what on Earth is this thing?" she asked with a hint of bemusement in her voice. Ethan grinned.

"That is a genuine 'Springpedalatron.' Back in the day, people used it for a combination of exercise and entertainment. It's like the precursor to a pogo stick. Wanna give it a whirl?"

Jessica laughed and declined, but the idea of a Springpedalatron workout entertained the group as his designs and notions usually did. His cousin, Alex, who had just returned from a backpacking trip, eyed a shelf filled with vintage compasses.

"Ethan, I get that you love history, but isn't this a bit much?" he quipped.

Ethan pretended to consider the question seriously.

"Well, you see, Alex, it's all about being prepared. If the GPS satellites ever go haywire, I've got enough compasses to lead an expedition across uncharted territories!"

The room erupted in laughter, but there was an undeniable charm in Ethan's genuine enthusiasm for his collection. As the evening continued, Sandra, Alex's girlfriend, noticed a peculiar-looking teapot on Ethan's kitchen counter. It was adorned with an assortment of mismatched buttons.

"Ethan, what's the story behind this teapot?"

"Don't set him off again," groaned Alex as they all laughed.

Ethan chuckled, pouring tea into mismatched cups.

"Ah, that teapot has a rich history. It belonged to a quirky inventor who believed that buttons held the power to unlock creativity. Legend has it, every time you brew tea in this teapot, you come up with the most brilliant ideas."

Sandra raised an eyebrow, clearly intrigued.

"And has it worked for you?"

Ethan grinned sheepishly.

"After a few batches, I realized my AI tea processor does a much better job than I ever could. Besides, I got sick of wasting tea."

Later that evening, as Ethan's friends bid their farewells, Jessica patted him on the back, teasingly saying,

"Ethan, you sure know how to keep things interesting, albeit a little geeky!"

He smiled warmly, his eyes glinting with enthusiasm. "Life should always have a touch of the unexpected, don't you think? History is what will bring the future."

Little did Ethan know that he was going to go from studying history to being a part of it soon.

Chapter 1: The Chronos Resurgence

Ethan had always been drawn to the pull of exploration, but his life in Prime Meridian had become a monotonous routine of work, deadlines, and the ceaseless hum of the city. However, a glimmer of excitement had recently ignited within him when he stumbled upon an intriguing thread on an online forum he frequented. It was a cryptic message hinting at the existence of an abandoned research facility, concealed by layers of history and forgotten by time. Though there was no way of being certain if it was real or simply an internet rumor, the prospect of uncovering something extraordinary filled him with an irresistible sense of adventure.

With each passing day, the idea of the hidden research facility gnawed at him, beckoning him to break free from the confines of his ordinary existence. He decided to embark on a quest to find it. Armed with a backpack, a flashlight, a hoverboard, and a tinge of skepticism, Ethan set out on a crisp Saturday morning, venturing to the outskirts of Prime Meridian, where the coordinates from the forum had led him. The landscape was a stark contrast to the city's bustling streets. It was where nature had begun to reclaim its territory. As he pushed through a thicket of underbrush and followed a winding path, there was a hidden downward descent leading to a shadowed area.

At first, he thought of turning back due to the sharp incline, but with a heavy breath of determination, he sat down at the top and skidded his way down. He reached the bottom of a tangled mess and realized quickly why no one else had found this place before. Also, because the others on the forums were nerds like him who preferred talking about adventures rather than experiencing them, they were the ones who never left the comforts of the Prime Meriden enclosure.

It was a miracle he didn't die coming down, he thought, brushing the dirt off his knee, accidentally smearing blood along it. He made a mental note to disinfect the wound later as he entered the ruins of the old research facility. It was an awe-inspiring sight, a sprawling complex of crumbling interiors and alcoves that seemed to have once been a hub of scientific inquiry.

The facility's main building stood like a sentinel, its windows long shattered, and its façade weathered by decades of exposure to the elements. Vines and moss covered the cracked concrete walls, adding to its hidden appearance. Ethan's excitement grew with each step. He couldn't believe his luck. The online forum had seemed like a mere curiosity, but here he stood on the threshold of a real-life adventure. He was about to enter a place untouched by time, a relic of the past waiting to be uncovered.

With cautious steps, he entered the main building. The interior was shrouded in darkness, the only source of light coming from the narrow beams of sunlight filtering through the cracks in the ceiling and sides. The air was thick with the combined scent of decay and growing grass. He soon made out that the place was a laboratory, a place where scientists had once conducted experiments that were now lost to oblivion. Broken glassware lay strewn across the floor, and faded chalkboards bore equations that had long lost their meaning. Ethan moved deeper into the facility, his flashlight cutting through the darkness. Each corner held its own secrets—a bookshelf with dust-covered books, a corner with rotting wooden benches, and a series of interconnected corridors that seemed to lead even further underground. As he explored further, he stumbled upon what appeared to be a control room. An array of buttons, switches, and dials were sprawled over a massive console that occupied the center of the chamber. His heart raced as he realized the significance of this discovery. It was a control room for something, *but what?* With trembling hands, he began to inspect the controls. To his amazement, some of the instruments still glowed faintly, as if they were waiting for someone to breathe life into them once more. His mind raced with possibilities—what kind of research had been conducted here, and what could this control room have overseen? The hours slipped away unnoticed as he traversed the labyrinthine corridors, guided by his insatiable curiosity and the flickering beam of his flashlight.

It was in a secluded chamber Ethan's heart swelled with exhilaration. He marveled at the serendipity of it all—the chance discovery of a hidden research facility, the tantalizing mysteries it held, and the opportunity to unravel its secrets. It was a moment that defied the monotony of his daily life, a moment when he stood at the crossroads of history and the unknown.

That was when he saw the faint glow in the darkness. Ethan was dumbfounded as he stood before the mysterious artifact. He felt the irresistible urge to touch it, reach out, and feel it. His fingertips brushed against the cool, metallic surface of the artifact. It responded with a faint, pulsating hum as if it recognized his presence and welcomed his curiosity. The light from the attached crystalline pieces seemed to glow brighter and brighter. A shiver coursed through him, and he pressed his hand against it, his skin making contact with the intricate patterns etched into the metal. Reality seemed to twist and contort around him, like a surreal dream unfolding in slow motion. The room dissolved into a swirling vortex of light and motion, and Ethan felt suddenly dizzy. It was as if the boundaries of time and space had blurred, and he was no longer bound by the laws of the physical world. The kaleidoscope of colors and patterns enveloped him, a mesmerizing dance of light that defied description. It was as if he were hurtling through the cosmos, a passenger on a voyage through the very fabric of existence. Time lost all meaning. The sensation was both exhilarating and disorienting.

Ethan had the distinct feeling of being suspended in a realm that transcended human comprehension. He couldn't discern up from down, left from right, as the patterns of light and motion continued to swirl around him. Then, just as suddenly as it had begun, the chaotic dance of colors and patterns came to an abrupt halt. Ethan's feet touched solid ground, and he found himself standing in a place he could not recognize. The transition was seamless, and he felt as though he had been deposited in a new reality with no clear reference point.

He could feel the ground beneath his feet shift as Ethan's mind raced to make sense of it all, to comprehend the nature of the world he now found himself in. He had longed for the unknown, but this was beyond anything he could have imagined. As he stood on that rocky plateau, bathed in the bright sunlight of this unknown world before his eyesight shifted back into focus. He heard an almost deafening roar and quickly ran to hide behind the closest towering tree as he came to terms with what he was seeing around him.

All prehistoric life in all its primal glory engulfed him. Beyond the safety of his refuge, this ancient time came alive with sights and sounds that defied his wildest imagination. Amidst the dense foliage, he witnessed a fierce battle between two gigantic behemoths—a Tyrannosaurus rex and a massive Sauropod. The earth shook as the titans clashed, their roars of fury and agony reverberating through the forest. The T. rex, with its serrated teeth gleaming in the sunlight, lunged at the Sauropod's massive neck while the herbivore retaliated with powerful sweeps of its tail. It was a brutal, primeval struggle for survival or death that had played out for millions of years.

Ethan watched in awe as the battle unfolded, the ground trembling beneath his feet with each thunderous impact. The sheer scale of these prehistoric creatures was staggering. As the dinosaurs clashed, a flock of pterosaurs soared through the skies above, their membranous wings spanning great distances. Their graceful forms cut through the air like avian acrobats, and Ethan stared open-jawed at their aerial maneuvers. These winged reptiles, with their beaks and toothless jaws, were a stark contrast to the terrestrial giants below.

With a wingspan that seemed to stretch to the horizon, one particularly large pterosaur glided past Ethan with majestic grace. Its leathery wings created a rush of air that rustled the leaves around him, and for a moment, he felt as though he was done for. As the battle between the T. Rex and the sauropod raged on, Ethan contemplated his predicament. He had been transported to a time when humans did not exist when the rules of nature were defined by a different set of laws. The artifact that had brought him here was nowhere to be found, and he had no way of knowing if it even existed in this distant past. The urgency of his situation weighed on him. He needed to find a way back.

Ethan took a cautious step away from his hiding place, his eyes scanning the horizon for any sign of the artifact or a clue that could guide him. The prehistoric world stretched out before him, a vast and untamed wilderness that held both wonder and peril. As he ventured a little deeper into the ancient forest, the distant cries of other dinosaurs echoed through the trees. He encountered herds of ornithopods, their graceful forms grazing on prehistoric ferns, and small, nimble predators that darted through the underbrush in search of prey. These herbivorous dinosaurs, with their graceful, bird-like appearances, had always fascinated him when he saw them in history books and the prehistoric museum back at Prime Meridien. Now, he found himself in their midst, a visitor from a distant future. Curiosity seemed to be mutual as the ornithopods regarded him with a blend of cautious interest and wariness. Their long, slender necks craned to get a closer look at this strange intruder in their world. Ethan remained still, not wanting to alarm the gentle giants. Slowly, he extended a hand, palm open, toward the nearest ornithopod. To his astonishment, one of the dinosaurs approached cautiously, its eyes fixated on his outstretched hand. With great care, the ornithopod nuzzled Ethan's palm, its beak gentle and inquisitive. Ethan smiled as he realized that this ancient creature, millions of years removed from his own time, was reaching out to him in a gesture of curiosity and connection.

The other members of the herd soon followed suit, their inquisitiveness piqued by the interaction. Ethan found himself surrounded by these prehistoric beings, their warm breaths and soft nuzzles unassuming and harmless. For a brief moment, as he stood amidst the ornithopods, Ethan felt a profound sense of connection to this ancient world. Yet, despite the awe-inspiring sights and this interaction, Ethan could not shake the overwhelming sense of panic and anxiety that had begun to take hold of him now that the adrenaline of his new surroundings and his encounter seemed to be wearing off—how was he going to get back? How could he find a way to return to the life he had left behind? That was when he saw the glow, first faintly and then brighter and brighter until he was completely blinded by it.

Chapter 2: The Future Within the Past

As the blinding light faded and Ethan's vision slowly cleared, he saw a woman standing in front of him, her presence both enigmatic and commanding. She was clad in a sleek, form-fitting uniform that seemed to shimmer with a subtle luminescence, mirroring the lights that had flashed around him when he touched the device. Her dark hair cascaded down her shoulders in waves, and her eyes, a striking shade of deep blue, held an intensity that seemed to pierce his very soul. Sarah, as she introduced herself, regarded Ethan with a mix of curiosity and recognition. Her authoritative demeanor hinted at a level of knowledge and experience that far exceeded his own. She extended a hand, her touch firm and reassuring as if she were a guide in this bewildering landscape.

"It's good to see you, Ethan," she said, her voice carrying a soothing reassurance. "I've been expecting you."

Ethan's mind raced with a whirlwind of questions, but before he could articulate them, Sarah began to speak, revealing a connection that left him stunned.

"You see, Ethan," Sarah explained, her voice carrying an air of mystery, "I have a deep connection to the Chronos Resurgence, the device you encountered before. It was created by my ancestors, a secretive group of scientists and explorers who sought to unlock the mysteries of time itself."

Ethan's disbelief was palpable as he struggled to comprehend the implications of her words. Time travel had been the stuff of science fiction and the wildest dreams of humanity, but here, in this prehistoric realm, it was becoming a reality before his very eyes. Sarah continued, her gaze never leaving his.

"The Chronos Resurgence has the power to traverse time, to journey to the distant past and the unknown future. It's a marvel of technology and ingenuity, and it holds the key to unlocking the secrets of the cosmos."

"How is this possible?" he whispered, his voice barely audible amidst the roar and clash of sounds around them. "How can something like time travel exist?"

Sarah smiled, motioning to their surroundings and the prehistoric creatures that flew overhead. "It exists, Ethan. There are those who dared to dream and push the boundaries of human knowledge. The Chronos Resurgence is a testament to the unyielding spirit of exploration and discovery."

As he looked at Sarah, with her authoritative presence and her connection to the Chronos Resurgence, he realized that the mysterious artifact had opened the door to a world of possibilities. Sarah's words hung in the air, and as Ethan absorbed the profound implications of their meeting, he felt a sense of awe and trepidation. He also began to feel sick. Sarah seemed unfazed. "We maintain the timeline, save the world. That sort of thing."

Before Ethan had a chance to respond, their conversation was interrupted by a sudden, bone-chilling roar. Ethan's heart leaped into his throat, and he instinctively stepped back, his eyes widening in terror. Out of the dense foliage, a colossal, predatory dinosaur emerged, its massive form casting a shadow over them. Its jagged teeth gleamed with malevolent intent, and its eyes burned with an insatiable hunger. Panic surged through Ethan as he watched the immense predator draw nearer, its steps shaking the ground with each thunderous footfall. He had heard about the incredible size and power of dinosaurs, but facing one in the flesh was an entirely different experience—one that filled him with a paralyzing fear.

Sarah, on the other hand, reacted with a level of composure that left Ethan in shock. With cool, unflinching precision, she drew a sleek, futuristic laser weapon from her side holster. The weapon shimmered with a faint luminescence, its design a testament to advanced technology. In an instant that felt like an eternity, Sarah took aim with her High Energy laser (HEL) pistol and fired a focused beam of energy at the charging dinosaur. The blast struck the creature square in the chest, and the result was nothing short of astonishing. The dinosaur disintegrated into a cloud of shimmering particles, leaving only the echo of its roar in the air.

Ethan stood frozen in place, his eyes locked on the spot where the colossal predator had once stood. He had witnessed the incredible power of Sarah's weapon, and it left him both amazed and terrified. Sarah holstered her (HEL) pistol with practiced ease, her demeanor unshaken by the life-or-death encounter. She turned to Ethan with a calm expression, her eyes holding a glimmer of amusement.

"Welcome to the dangers of the past, Ethan," she said, her voice carrying a hint of wry humor. "You're lucky I was here to protect you."

Ethan nodded, still trying to process what had just happened. After the dust settled and the echoes of the encounter faded into the background, Sarah continued their conversation. "I would like to extend an invitation to you. You have seen the power of the Chronos Resurgence, and you have glimpsed the mysteries of time itself. I invite you to join the Temporal Defense Corp, a secret organization dedicated to safeguarding the timeline and exploring the boundless possibilities of time travel."

The prospect of becoming part of an organization tasked with such a monumental responsibility was both exhilarating and daunting. He thought about the potential for discovery and the chance to unravel the secrets of time but could not seem to focus his alignment or thoughts on all that was happening. Sarah seemed to understand the turmoil in his thoughts. "I can see that this is a lot to take in, Ethan," she said, her tone empathetic. "But know that the Temporal Defense Corp are the guardians of time itself, and we have the knowledge and technology to navigate its complexities safely. You wouldn't be alone in this journey."

Ethan nodded, gratitude and uncertainty warring within him. He appreciated the offer and the guidance Sarah had provided, but he needed time to process everything. With a reassuring smile, Sarah stepped closer to Ethan. "Look, just think about it," she said. "For now, I'll help you return to your own time. If you decide to join us, I'll be there to guide you through what comes next."

Sarah walked over to the spot she had first appeared in. With a few deft movements, she activated a holographic interface that projected a swirling vortex of light. She turned back to Ethan. "All you need to do is think about your time and place, and the

Chronos Resurgence will take you there," Sarah explained. "When you're ready, just step into the vortex."

As he stepped closer to the swirling vortex of light, he turned to Sarah. "Thank you, Sarah, for saving my life," he said, his voice filled with sincerity.

With those parting words, Ethan stepped into the vortex, and the landscape around him began to dissolve. He closed his eyes, and time once again seemed to flow around him, carrying him back to the abandoned laboratory in his own time as he materialized in the familiar surroundings. Ethan looked down and saw the Chronos Resurgence lying at his feet. He hesitated for a moment, then cautiously picked up the device and placed it in his backpack.

Ethan's solitary journey back home was filled with the kind of quiet reflection that only comes after experiencing the extraordinary. The hoverboard glided effortlessly over the terrain, carrying him up the steep incline that led to the abandoned science lab. The memories of the ancient past, the surreal realm, and his encounter with Sarah raced through his mind like a vivid dream.

As he entered his modest home filled with his trinkets and gadgets, he felt a sense of detachment from the mundane routines of his everyday life. The contrast between the astonishing experiences of the past few hours and the familiarity of his surroundings was jarring, and it left him in a state of contemplation. Ethan stepped into the shower, the warm water washing away the dust that clung to him. It was a moment of solitude, a chance to collect his thoughts and come to terms with the revelations that had unfolded before him. He quickly disinfected his wound and covered it with a 'Quick-Heal' bandage so that it would be gone by the next morning.

Afterward, he made a simple sandwich, his hands mechanically moving as he assembled the ingredients. First turkey, then cheese, then mayo, all put together. Easy and filling, it was his go-to when he was too tired to cook anything properly. As he sat down at the kitchen table, sandwich in hand, he allowed his thoughts to shift back to the Chronos Resurgence. He had taken it home as per Sarah's instructions, and it lay nearby, a silent testament to the mysteries of time and the boundless possibilities that now rested in his possession. The device's glow seemed to flicker with a promise of adventures yet to come. He cleaned up and made his way to his bedroom.

Climbing into bed, Ethan felt a sense of exhaustion wash over him. The events of the day had taken a toll on both his body and his mind. As he pulled the covers over himself, he wondered about the choices that lay ahead. The Chronos Resurgence remained a tantalizing enigma that illuminated the darkness of the unknown and an uncertain possibility of something great. With each passing moment, as sleep began to calm him, Ethan knew his mind was still trapped in a mesh of confusion.

What if he were to use the Chronos Resurgence to change the course of history? What if he could prevent calamities, alter the fates of individuals, or reshape the world to his liking? The possibilities were boundless, and it was this boundlessness that troubled him the most. But as his mind ventured deeper into these thoughts, he realized the profound ethical dilemmas that such power presented. The consequences of altering history were far-reaching and unpredictable. What might seem like a noble act in one era could lead to unforeseen catastrophes in another. He couldn't escape the gravity of the responsibility that lay before him. The power to manipulate time was a double-edged sword, capable of both great good and unimaginable harm. The decisions he made could reverberate across the ages, affecting countless lives and shaping the destiny of humanity itself. In the silence of his room, he grappled with the moral quandaries that swirled within him. What right did he have to tamper with the intricacies of time? Who was he to decide which events should be altered and which should be preserved? It was a burden that weighed heavily on his conscience. And yet, there was another side to his inner conflict. Ethan dared not deny the allure of discovery and exploration that the Chronos Resurgence represented. The mysteries of the past, the enigmas of the future—they called to him with an irresistible pull.

Ethan knew that the Chronos Resurgence was a tool, neither inherently good nor evil. It was the intentions and actions of those who wielded it that would determine its impact on history.

With this realization, he made a silent vow to himself. He would use the knowledge he had gained responsibly to protect the course of history rather than disrupt it. He would learn from the past, study the future, and ensure that the power of time remained a force for preservation rather than manipulation. As he closed his eyes and drifted into the realm of dreams, his mind was filled with a sense of purpose and determination. The mysteries of time were his to explore, but he would do so with a deep respect for the integrity of history itself.

He decided he would join the Temporal Defense Corp.

Chapter 3: Temporal Defense Corps

The Temporal Defense Corps (TDC) Headquarters stood as a beacon of advanced technology and historical knowledge. This sprawling complex, nestled in a tucked away part of Meridian, was a sanctuary where the past, present, and future converged in an expansive paradigm. The exterior of the TDC Headquarters was a testament to modern design and innovation. Gleaming towers and arching bridges stretched toward the sky, adorned with intricate patterns that paid homage to the eras of human history. The blend of architectural styles from across the ages created a visually stunning contrast to the azure sky behind it.

As Ethan entered the grand foyer, he was greeted by the sight of a colossal, holographic globe suspended in mid-air. This globe displayed a mesmerizing collage of historical events, each one a ripple in the river of time. It was a reminder that the past, the present, and the future were all connected, and the TDC was the guardian of that connection. The corridors of the TDC Headquarters walls exhibited holographic displays of historical data, timelines, and events. The air buzzed with the soft hum of futuristic machinery, and overhead, levitating transport pods glided effortlessly, ferrying personnel to their destinations. Within the heart of the headquarters was the Temporal Archives, an expansive repository of knowledge that spanned the annals of time. Gigantic, illuminated screens displayed historical documents, artifacts, and interactive holographic displays that allowed visitors to journey through pivotal moments in history.

Ethan found himself surrounded by experts and scholars from diverse fields, their knowledge spanning centuries. Historians, scientists, archaeologists, and explorers worked side by side, each one dedicated to preserving the integrity of the timeline and uncovering its hidden secrets. The Temporal Command Center was a nerve center of activity, a vast, circular chamber filled with rows of sophisticated consoles. Agents in sleek uniforms monitored screens that displayed the temporal flux, tracking disturbances and anomalies in time. A holographic representation of the timeline hung in the center of the room, a web of interconnected threads representing the sections of the past, present, and future.

The heart of the Temporal Command Center was the Timegate Chamber, an imposing structure of gleaming metal and crystalline technology. It was a portal that allowed access to different eras, a gateway to time itself. This chamber was under the strictest security, with guards and advanced biometric scanners ensuring that only authorized personnel could access its power. The knowledge and technology at their disposal were awe-inspiring, and it was clear that their responsibilities extended far beyond the present. They were stewards of time, protecting the past and safeguarding the future. In a secluded chamber known as the Sanctum of Preservation, Ethan discovered an overwhelming collection of artifacts from different points in history. Ancient scrolls, priceless relics, and technological wonders were displayed with meticulous care, each one a witness to the diversity and richness of human history. Being an avid collector of historical artifacts, his jaw was left hanging on the floor at this never-ending collection.

The Sanctum of Preservation was more than a museum; it was a living testament to the importance of preserving the past. He could sense the weight of history in this room, the echoes of countless lives and events that had shaped the world. He encountered the members of the TDC, individuals from various backgrounds who shared a common commitment to the organization's mission. They were bound by a deep reverence for the mysteries of time and a profound respect for the responsibility they bore. He realized that he could be part of something far greater than himself, a mission that transcended individual desires and ambitions. The mysteries of time were vast and complex, and the TDC was at the forefront of unraveling those ambiguities.

Ethan was informed that his time there was not just about the knowledge he gained; it was also about the rigorous training that would prepare him for the responsibilities that came with wielding the power of the Chronos Resurgence. The training was intense and comprehensive, a mix of physical endurance, mental acuity, and mastery of time manipulation technology. Every day brought new challenges, pushing Ethan to his limits as he sought to become proficient in the use of the Chronos Resurgence. One of his trainers was a seasoned agent named Captain Reynolds, a no-nonsense, straight-shooting instructor known for his stringent approach to training. He was a man who had seen it all, and he had little patience for those who didn't take their responsibilities seriously. One day, during an exercise in the TDC training facility, Captain Reynolds gathered the trainees for a practical demonstration of time manipulation. The exercise involved retrieving an artifact from a specific moment in history and returning it to the present. Ethan and his fellow trainees stood before Timegate, which had a holographic interface that displayed the timeline. They each had their own Time travel device, a smaller and more manageable version that interacted with the Timegate, similar to the Chronos Resurgence Ethan had encountered in the abandoned laboratory.

"Listen up, recruits," Captain Reynolds barked, his voice commanding attention. "Today, we're going to practice retrieving an artifact from the past. Remember, precision and timing are everything in this line of work. We don't want any unexpected historical disturbances."

The holographic interface displayed a series of historical events, each marked with a holographic representation of an artifact. The trainees were tasked with selecting a specific moment and retrieving the designated artifact. Ethan was determined to excel in this exercise. He had spent hours studying historical events and had honed his understanding of how to use the Chronos Resurgence. With a steely resolve, he selected a moment in ancient Egypt where the artifact was marked as an ancient scroll. As he initiated the retrieval process, he could feel the power of the Chronos Resurgence at his fingertips. The sensation was exhilarating as if he held the tendrils of time in his grasp. The artifact materialized in his hand, an ancient scroll, and he knew that he had successfully completed the exercise. But just as he was about to celebrate his achievement, Captain Reynolds' stern voice cut through the air. "Hold on, recruit. Let's see what you've got."

Ethan approached the instructor, the ancient scroll in hand. "I've retrieved the artifact, sir."

Captain Reynolds eyed him with a critical gaze. "Let's see if you've got it right. Unroll that scroll."

 Unrolling the ancient document with the utmost care, he looked at its delicate, weathered pages. The content was written in hieroglyphics, an ancient Egyptian script. He knew that deciphering it was accurately crucial. Captain Reynolds raised an eyebrow and glanced at the hieroglyphics. "Well, recruit, are you going to translate that for us, or did you just bring back a souvenir from the past?"

Ethan's heart sank. He hadn't anticipated the need to translate the ancient text on the spot. He frantically searched his memory for the meanings of the hieroglyphics, his face turning a shade of crimson just as the pressure was mounting. Sarah, who had become his mentor of sorts and was watching the exercise, chimed in with a mischievous grin. "Come on, kid, I thought you were the history buff here. You didn't think we'd let you off that easy, did you?"

He was being tested and chuckled at the situation. He took a deep breath, suppressing his embarrassment, and began to decipher the hieroglyphics to the best of his ability. The assembled agents watched with amusement as he stumbled through the translation, misinterpreting a few symbols along the way. Captain Reynolds finally allowed a small smile to crease his stern expression. "Not bad, recruit. You may have some work to do on your hieroglyphics, but at least you've got a sense of humor. Remember, precision in time travel means more than just retrieving artifacts. It means understanding the context and the impact those artifacts have on history."

His embarrassment was quickly replaced with a sense of determination. The exercise was a valuable lesson in the complexities of time manipulation, and he was eager to learn from his mistakes. As the training continued, he embraced the challenges as well as the camaraderie that came with being a part of the Temporal Defense Corps. He knew that he was on a path filled with uncertainties and ethical dilemmas, but with each day of training, he was one step closer to becoming a guardian of time, ready to protect the course of history and navigate the complexities of time with wisdom and resolve. Sarah had taken on the role of guiding him through the details of being a member of the Temporal Defense Corps. She was a figure of authority and experience, someone who had walked the line between preserving history and the tantalizing temptation to alter it. Their training often involved observing pivotal moments in history, and it was during these experiences that Sarah emphasized the delicate balance of the timeline. As they stood together in the Temporal Observation Chamber, a colossal, spherical room filled with holographic interfaces, Ethan couldn't help but feel a sense of awe. The holographic displays shifted and swirled, revealing scenes from different eras and events that had shaped the course of humanity.

Sarah stood beside him, her eyes filled with a profound respect for the mysteries of time. "Listen to me," she began, her voice carrying a weight of responsibility, "The key to being a guardian of time is understanding the impact of every moment in history. We must tread carefully, for even the smallest alteration can send ripples through time."

There were many things he could have looked at, but his gaze was fixed on the holographic display that now showcased a pivotal moment—the signing of the Declaration of Independence. He watched as the Founding Fathers penned their names on the historic document, the birth of a nation taking shape before him. The moment was a testament to the courage and vision of those who had paved the way for a new era of freedom. The weight of their actions was palpable, and Ethan could sense the profound impact it had on the course of history. Sarah continued their journey through time, and the next scene depicted the Wright brothers' first powered flight. The grainy footage showed Orville and Wilbur Wright as they achieved the impossible, lifting off the ground and ushering in the age of aviation.

To witness the audacity of the Wright brothers, their unwavering determination to defy gravity, and the lasting impact their invention would have on the world was beyond Ethan's wildest dreams. It was a moment that spoke of human ingenuity and the boundless possibilities of progress. As they moved through time, he observed moments that left an indelible mark on his understanding of history. The fall of the Berlin Wall, the moon landing, and the colonizing of the moon—all of these events served as reminders of the profound impact of human actions on the course of time. But it was during the observation of the signing of the Emancipation Proclamation that he felt a wave of emotion wash over him. The holographic display showed President Abraham Lincoln putting pen to paper, a symbol of hope and liberation for countless individuals.

It was so visceral that he truly felt he understood the significance of this moment in the struggle for equality and justice. The bravery it took to stand against the currents of history and declare the end of slavery was hard proof of the power of a single decision — a decision that shaped the course of a nation. Sarah turned to him, her eyes reflecting the gravity of the moment. "Ethan, every moment in history is a fragile thread in the tapestry of time. Our duty is to protect that and ensure that it remains intact. The power we hold with the Chronos Resurgence is a double-edged sword, and we must wield it with caution and wisdom."

He nodded, his heart filled with a newfound understanding of the responsibilities that came with being a guardian of time. The delicate balance of the timeline was a weighty responsibility, and he was determined to honor it. The balance of the timeline was a delicate dance, and he was ready to step into that dance with a profound respect for the past, the present, and the future. The responsibility of a guardian of time was not to alter history but to preserve it, to protect the collection of human experiences, and to ensure that its threads remained unbroken.

Chapter 4: Zin Xia

As Ethan prepared for his upcoming mission to Ancient China, he delved into extensive research, studying the historical context and the specific events that required correction in the timeline. The Temporal Defense Corps had identified a critical juncture in that period and location, making it their responsibility to ensure that the course of history remained unaltered. He spent countless hours poring over holographic records, historical texts, and visual simulations. Every detail had to be precise, and every action had to be well-planned. It was his biggest mission yet.

It was during one of his research sessions that he stumbled upon a holographic record that left him confused. The record depicted a woman named Zin Xia, a figure who was not part of the mission of the ancient Chinese timeline correction he was preparing for. She stood as a towering figure of strength and resilience, a warrior and scholar whose legacy had remained hidden in the annals of history. Why hadn't Ethan heard of her before? He loved the Ancient Chinese civilization and thought his in-depth knowledge of that period was why he was selected for this particular mission, but then how could he have missed all about this woman? Ethan watched in rapt fascination as the holographic projection brought Zin Xia to life.

She was clad in armor, a sword at her side, with a fierceness in her eyes that pierced through him even though he was only looking at a collection of light particles from eons ago. The hologram displayed scenes from her life, painting a vivid portrait of someone who had defied the norms of her era. Zin Xia was an academic like him, well-versed in the ancient texts and philosophies of China. She had mastered the arts of calligraphy and poetry, her intellect matching the speed of her sword on the battlefield. The holographic record showed her leading armies into battle with a battle cry that visibly shook fear into her enemies' forces. She was not just a warrior; she was a strategist, a leader, and a symbol of hope in a world that sought to confine her.

Ethan felt a deep sense of admiration for Zin Xia, but as he continued to watch the holographic record, he realized that Zin Xia's life was not without its challenges. The society of her time had placed stringent limitations on the roles and expectations of women. Yet, she had shattered those constraints; being the only child of her parents, she carved a path of her own and filled the roles her father wanted for his imagined son. Because of this, she had a notable chip on her shoulder that was evident even through these briefs etches of her life. This particular holographic record ended with an image of Zin Xia standing on a mountaintop. Her sword raised high, alone yet powerful. Ethan was left in awe of the woman he had just discovered, unable to pull away from the wonder of why her legacy had remained hidden for so long.

With renewed determination, Ethan continued his preparations, his heart filled with a deep sense of respect for Zin Xia and a profound commitment to preserving the timeline. The mysteries of history were vast and complex, and he was certain there was more to this tale than met the eye, but he wouldn't allow himself to get distracted right then, not with so much on the line. Not when he had so much to prove.

The day of the reconnaissance missions to Ancient China had arrived, and Ethan found himself in the equipment room, surrounded by an array of futuristic safety gear. He had been meticulously trained in its usage, but as he attempted to put on the gear, he felt a wave of uncertainty wash over him. Sarah, who was overseeing the preparations, tried to suppress a mischievous grin but failed as she watched him struggle with the gear. As he was holding up a piece of the gear, a complex-looking helmet with multiple adjustable straps, he frowned. He examined it as if it were an alien artifact, wondering how he could blank out about how it worked. He prided himself on his memory and understanding of technology, being one of the top rookies on his team.

"Sarah," he began, his voice tinged with frustration, "I think I might need a manual for this." Sarah chuckled and approached him, her own gear perfectly in place. "Come on, rookie, it's not rocket science. Put the helmet on your head, secure the straps, and you're good to go." Ethan shot her a dubious look.

"Are you sure about that? It looks like there are more straps here than in my entire shoe collection. And for the life of me, I can't remember what these three knobs do," Sarah bellowed with laughter. "Trust me, you'll get the hang of it. Just follow my lead."

As Ethan reluctantly placed the helmet on his head, he began to fumble with the straps. It was like watching someone try to solve a Rubik's Cube for the first time. The straps twisted and turned, creating a labyrinth of confusion.

Sarah couldn't contain her amusement any longer, "It's like watching a baby elephant take its first steps. Here, let me help you. I beg." She reached over and deftly adjusted the straps, securing the helmet in place before turning the knobs to the right setting.

"Thanks. I think I'll get the hang of it. Eventually,"

He then moved on to the next piece of gear—a futuristic jumpsuit with multiple zippers and clasps. He held it up, his expression a mix of skepticism and resignation. "Okay, this should be easy," he muttered to himself. "It's just a jumpsuit. People wear these all the time."

But as he began to put on the jumpsuit, his struggles continued. He zipped it up the front, only to realize that it had two zippers, one on each side. He looked down at his front, then his back, then back at the jumpsuit, clearly confounded.

"The intricacies of Time Travel are at our disposal, and you can't even suit up. I'm beginning to worry," Sarah joked as she approached him and unzipped the jumpsuit, guiding him through the process with a playful grin. It was like watching a child learn to dress themselves for the first time, and Sarah's patience and humor made the process much more enjoyable. Instead of being embarrassed, he was amused by his own ineptitude.

"I have to admit, I'm starting to think that maybe I should stick to my old-fashioned clothes. They don't come with as many straps and zippers,"

Sarah patted his shoulder with a reassuring smile. "Don't worry. I took three months to learn how to start up the ground cart transportation vehicle, and it's literally just two buttons that say 'on' and 'off.' You'll get the hang of it. Besides, I think you'll look quite dashing in that jumpsuit when it's on right. Very Men in Black"

"Next, you'll be telling me aliens are real, too."

"The way you look right now, I don't think we're that far off from admitting to their existence."

With the safety gear finally in place, Ethan and Sarah made their way to the mission briefing room, readying for the next stage in their preparation. The earlier moments of confusion and laughter had eased the tension, and they both knew that they were prepared for whatever challenges lay ahead. He had faith in his training, and Sarah had developed faith in him through it. The mysteries of time were vast and complex, but with a mentor like her, he felt like he owed it to be better than everyone else without taking life as seriously as he had before. She introduced him to a sort of lightheartedness he had never experienced before.

Continuing the preparation for the mission to Ancient China, he repeatedly found himself spellbound by the profound connection with Zin Xia. He couldn't help himself. It was as if her enigma consumed him — a moth to a flame that had long since been extinguished. The holographic record had opened a window to her world, and with every glimpse into her life, Ethan felt a magnetic pull that transcended the boundaries of time. He admired her tenacity and the fire that burned within her. The holographic images displayed scenes from Zin Xia's early life when her father expressed nothing but disappointment over her gender while simultaneously pushing her to train to the point where he thought she would break. But Zin Xia had been different. She had shown an insatiable hunger for knowledge, even as a young girl. The holographic record revealed her sitting in the corner of a dimly lit room, poring over ancient scrolls and texts, her eyes filled with a thirst for her father's approval as well as for knowledge.

It was a scene that resonated with Ethan, a reflection of his own love for exploration and learning. Zin Xia's journey was not limited to the world of knowledge. The holographic images showed her practicing martial arts with dedication and almost robotic discipline. She had embraced the physical and mental aspects of martial arts, mastering the art of combat with precision and grace. Ethan watched in awe as she engaged in a sparring match, her movements fluid and calculated. She was not just a warrior; she was a force to be reckoned with, a skilled martial artist who had honed her abilities with unwavering keenness under her father's watchful gaze. Ethan saw in her a kindred spirit, a fellow explorer despite the difference in their time periods. As he continued to study Zin Xia's life every chance he got, he felt guilt creep in. He should be using this time to prepare, but that was just not possible; his body and mind would not allow it. It was as if their paths were meant to intersect, even across the vast expanse of time. He knew that this was more than a simple curiosity as it was almost time for them to depart, but he was equally helpless and hopeless in his feelings. It was like when he was a kid and first learned that dinosaurs roamed the earth. For months, it was all he could think about — to say that he was *obsessed* was putting it mildly.

Sarah noticed Ethan's wanderings. The time he spent researching Zin Xia and how he would sneak off to the holographic records department any chance he got. She approached him one day, her expression softer than usual.

"Ethan," she began, "your passion for history is commendable, but remember that our role is to observe, to protect the timeline without interference."

Ethan nodded, acknowledging her words. He realized the importance of maintaining the delicate balance of history. Yet, the pull of Zin Xia's story was stronger than ever, no matter how much his logical brain tried to pull him away. And it was nearly time to go back to the time when she lived and breathed.

Chapter 5: Echoes of Ancient China

Ethan's determination to unravel the mystery of Zin Xia had become an all-encompassing fire burning brightly within him. He couldn't shake the feeling that he was being drawn to her for a reason — a reason that eluded him. The magnetic pull toward her story had become more than a passing curiosity; it felt like an integral part of his journey within the Temporal Defense Corps. It had to do with the reason he first stumbled across the Chronos Resurgence.

One day, after training sessions, he approached Sarah with an intensity in his eyes that immediately caught her attention. "Sarah, I need your help. I can't shake this feeling that Zin Xia's story is calling to me. I know the rules. I understand the balance, but I just… I need to understand why." He concluded simply, letting his hands drop to his side as he was frustrated; he couldn't better explain his feelings.

Sarah studied him for a moment, her expression completely unreadable. "We have our responsibilities as guardians of time. Delving into personal quests can be risky." She said, carefully measuring her words.

"I know, I know," he replied with a shrug, "But you've got to trust me on this one. There's more to it. I know it in my bones."

Sarah sighed, knowing she was fighting a losing battle by the look in his eye. "Fine, I'll help, but we need to be careful. We can't let personal pursuits compromise our mission or the timeline."

With a nod of gratitude, they delved into collaborative research, the TDC archives becoming their virtual playground. They scoured ancient texts, decrypted encrypted messages, and sifted through historical fragments to piece together the puzzle of Zin Xia's existence. The more they uncovered, the more the pieces seemed to fall into place. Zin Xia's life was a figment of brilliance and mystery, her story in pieces, only whispers of her ghost seen through time. As they deciphered encrypted messages that hinted at her location, the unspoken elephant in the room pertaining to the coincidence of their mission being in Ancient China was growing larger and larger.

"Could it be that Zin Xia is the key to our mission?" Ethan blurted out one day, unable to contain the excitement bubbling within him after they found a beautiful painting of Zin Xia in an old, forgotten record.

Sarah raised an eyebrow. "Or maybe it's just a cosmic coincidence. The universe works in mysterious ways. The only thing clear is time."

But he recognized the feeling that there was more to it. The encrypted messages they uncovered seemed to guide them toward the very location they were preparing to visit—Ancient China. The convergence of their mission and the pursuit of Zin Xia's story felt like more than chance. As they continued their research, the pieces of the puzzle fell into place with surprising synchronicity. They discovered coded messages within ancient scrolls, hints of Zin Xia's existence hidden in plain sight. The connections between their impending mission became undeniable. The timing, the location—it all seemed to align in a way that transcended mere coincidence.

"Listen to me. If there's a connection, we need to approach this with caution. Our primary responsibility is to the timeline. You still accept that as the universal truth of need, don't you?"

Ethan nodded, already having decided his loyalties lay with the timeline, no matter what the cost. As they prepared to embark on the mission, Ethan felt a mixture of anticipation and determination. The convergence of their personal quest and their duty as guardians of time had blurred the lines between destiny and responsibility.

The journey to Ancient China was in itself transcendent. As Ethan and Sarah stepped through the temporal rift, they found themselves immersed in a world of antiquity, a place where history breathed life into every corner. Their first steps led them to a bustling marketplace, a kaleidoscope of colors and sounds that overwhelmed the senses. Stalls adorned with silks and spices beckoned, their vibrant hues catching the sunlight filtering through the intricate lattice structures overhead. The air was thick with the mingling scents of exotic spices, the pungency of incense, and the earthy aroma of goods from distant lands.

Merchants, clad in richly embroidered garments, hawked their wares with animated voices that blended into a harmonious symphony of commerce. The clamor of bartering and the rhythmic clatter of wooden stalls being set up created a lively backdrop. The two of them stayed close and navigated the bustling thoroughfares, Ethan trying to keep up while not losing himself in the scenes unfolding around him.

Baskets of plump lychees and dragon fruits spilled over with abundance, while stalls with delicate patterns adorning porcelain vases and artifacts were near impossible for him to ignore. The scent of freshly steamed dumplings wafted through the air, tempting the passersby and making his stomach growl something fierce, even though he had had a hearty breakfast before they embarked on the mission. Street performers dressed in elaborate costumes added to the lively ambiance. Their movements synchronized with the rhythmic beats of drums and the melodic twang of traditional string instruments, captivating the attention of the crowd.

Amidst the vibrant chaos, ethereal beauty unfolded in tranquil gardens hidden behind carved gates. Courtyards adorned with blooming lotus flowers provided a sanctuary from the bustling marketplace. The gentle rustle of leaves and the soothing sounds of water flowing from ornate fountains created a serene backdrop, inviting contemplation in the midst of the ancient city's vibrancy. They cut through these peaceful oases, marveling at the delicate artistry of the architecture and the meticulous attention to detail in the garden layouts. Ancient stone pathways led them to pavilions where scholars once gathered, their conversations a melding of ideas interwoven with the fragrance of incense.

Their journey continued to ornate palaces, where towering pagodas reached the skyline, and halls adorned with vibrant murals depicted scenes of ancient battles, grand processions, and the flourishing arts surrounded them. Dragons, symbols of power and prosperity, danced across the walls, begging to be stared at. On more than a few occasions, Sarah had to tug at Ethan's sleeve and remind him to carry on as he stood transfixed. In the midst of the imperial city, echoes of traditional music emanated from ceremonial halls. The melodic tones of guqin and pipa instruments filled the air, and it would have been easy to get lost in their hypnotic rhythm.

High above the bustling city and serene gardens, they found themselves being led through their locator to a tea shop perched atop a mountain, surrounded by the graceful bend of a river. The air was thick with the calming scent of brewing tea, creating an ethereal smoke-filled aura that wrapped around them like an intoxicating embrace. The tea shop, with its weathered wooden beams and tables, exuded an atmosphere of calm. Large windows framed sweeping views of the landscape, showcasing the verdant slopes of the mountain and the meandering river below. The smoke from incense spiraled upward, casting a dreamlike haze that softened the edges of reality.

As they inspected the jars and ingredients, an old Chinese man emerged from the depths of the tea shop. He introduced himself as Li Wei, a local historian who, for reasons unknown, had anticipated their arrival. His attire reflected the traditional garments of ancient China, and his every movement seemed to be mirroring the fluidity of water. With a warm smile, he gestured for them to join him at a weathered wooden table adorned with delicate tea sets.

"I've been expecting you," Li Wei said, his voice a melodic whisper that blended seamlessly with the rustling leaves and the soft murmur of the river. "There are tales that echo through the mountains, whispers of seekers who journey to unravel the mysteries of the past."

"The mountains spread tales fairly fast then as we just arrived," Sarah told him with a cautious smile.

"You seek the story of Zin Xia, a woman whose spirit dances through the currents of time. Her tale is woven into the very fabric of this land, and I have walked the paths she treads."

The tea shop seemed to hold its breath, the smoke swirling in anticipation as Li Wei shared insights into the challenges faced by Zin Xia. He painted vivid pictures of her era, a time when societal norms confined the ambitions of women and the varying webs of relationships that had shaped her destiny.

He spoke of her pursuits in the martial arts, her hunger for knowledge, and the quiet rebellion against the constraints imposed by tradition. Li Wei hinted at the profound impact Zin Xia could have on the course of history. He spoke in riddles, his words a dance between past and present. Ethan and Sarah listened intently, noting down everything he said to analyze later.

Li Wei paused for a long moment before getting up to go to the window. He held out his hand, and after a minute, a chirping could be heard before a small yellow bird came and landed on his extended finger. The bird cocked his head, looking at the old man before it flew past him, inside the house to perch next to a ceramic bowl filled with tiny seeds. It pecked at them, occasionally stopping to whistle in the direction of Li Wei.

"The river of time flows, weaving the threads of countless stories. Zin Xia's legacy, like the river's bend, holds the power to shape the course of destiny. Seek with an open heart, and the answers you seek may reveal themselves in the currents of time. That is what you will need to face the 'Temporal Renegades.'"

"The Temporal Renegades?!" Sarah exclaimed, jumping out of her seat and disrupting the tranquility of their surroundings.

Ethan was taken aback. Usually, Sarah was so calm and collected that seeing her face contorted in what he could only understand to be fear was incredibly unsettling.

"Who are the Temporal Renegades?" Ethan asked as Li Wei calmly sipped his tea, clearly unphased by Sarah's outburst.

"Those who attempt to distort time for their own benefit," Lie Wei responded.

"A faction like that actually exists? How would we even go about finding them?"

Li Wei chuckled. " Lǔxíng Zhě (Traveler), I thought you knew. They are here. Now. In China. And they are being led by none other than Zin Xia."

Chapter 6: Threads Of Destiney

"Why do you think traces of her are like whispers of an echo with her life being louder than a battle cry? It is the duty of people like myself to remember her and honor her, even if she must forgo honoring herself," Li Wei said, adding the last part more softly.

"We have to go find her!" Ethan stated, standing up abruptly and almost knocking over the teacup that was placed in front of him.

"No. We must return to HQ. If what this man is telling us is true, we cannot approach her unarmed and with no plan or backup. The Temporal Renegades have taken down too many of our kind for us to go in without caution," Sarah responded, getting up herself. She bowed in the direction of Li Wei. "Thank you for your generosity and your time."

"Worry not; you will be back." He said, looking in Ethan's direction, who was still opening and closing his mouth without letting out a single sound. Li Wei bowed back as the two of them took their leave, Sarah pulling Ethan along as he tried to come up with reasons why they should stay after he found his voice again. He was only silenced when Sarah stopped and faced him.

"We need to re-group. Trust me," she stated before activating the time jump back to HQ. With their own time, they set about unraveling more layers of Zin Xia's story. Armed with the insights Li Wei had shared, they delved into the vast archives of the Temporal Defense Corps (TDC). That is when something strange happened. As they scoured scrolls and digital records, the name

Zin Xia appeared like a flickering flame, teasing them with traces of her history that seemed to dance on the edge of existence. Fragments of her life emerged, only to dissipate like mist, leaving behind echoes of a presence that defied the confines of linear time. Instances in history of what she did, however fleeting, were gone. Vanished. Even though Ethan could have sworn he had seen these with his own eyes, they were simply not there.

"We're going about this the wrong way. We need to start digging into all the information available about the Temporal Renegades instead of the TDC files," Sarah told him with a sigh.

"But I heard those change a lot because of the Renegades' interference with the timeline and that they weren't considered accurate so much, so they were locked from access."

"Live and learn, rookie," she told him with a grin, pulling out her all-access card. "Besides, Zin Xia is changing the TDC's current records of history, so we might as well try and dig out as much information as possible and then piece together the most plausible theories we can about her."

After accessing the Temporal Renegade files, Ethan and Sarah found themselves caught in a web of intrigue. The Temporal Renegades—a shadowy faction that aimed to manipulate time for their own benefit and greed were running rampant and always just out of the TDC's reach. Although a relatively new faction, they had managed to interfere with linear time to such an extent that the TDC put a kill-on-sight order out on them. They appeared when they were least expected and had already altered certain historical events so drastically that entire task forces of TDC needed to be assigned to the most seemingly benign moments in history to prevent major catastrophes. Butterfly Teams had to spend weeks, if not months, in a particular time zone, cleaning up after the Renegades.

Zin Xia had no more solidity in the restricted files than she did in the TDC archive. Her involvement appeared and disappeared like elusive phantoms, leaving behind half-clues that hinted at a deeper connection between her and the Renegades. The files seemed to warp around Zin Xia's history, defying the structured narrative of the past. Documents shifted, timelines blurred, and the very essence of her existence became a frustrating puzzle for them that resisted straightforward interpretation. Zin Xia's involvement with the Temporal Renegades created a narrative that transcended the conventional dichotomy of heroes and villains, and Ethan was even deeper down the rabbit hole of her life than ever. She began appearing in timelines of Ancient Greece, Egypt, and the Indus Civilization before vanishing and reappearing during the Tech Boom or Y2K.

"The more I know, the less I seem to understand about her," Ethan said with frustration, flicking a file of holographic records on the screen to the side with a swish of his wrist.

"We tried our best. I think you're right. We need to go face her and see if we can understand where she is coming from," Sarah responded, also switching off her monitor.

"Yes! That's what I've been saying. If we can speak to her face to face, I am sure she will help us understand why she is flitting between timelines with the Renegades and what they are hoping to achieve. We know for sure where she is and when; thanks to Li Wei, we can do this."

"Fine, but this time, there is no stopping at every stall with a pretty vase to sell. It was hard enough getting you to walk away from the Dumpling counter. We leave tomorrow morning, and we better come back with answers, or Command will have both our necks,"

"Deal," agreed Ethan as they got up and began packing up for the night.

The next day, earlier than the sunrise, they went back once more to Ancient China, where they were able to pinpoint Zin Xia's exact location with the help of Li Wei. His map led them to a hidden sanctuary nestled amidst the mountains, shrouded in a veil of secrecy. As they crisscrossed ancient pathways and concealed passages, the air hummed.

"How are you able to understand that scrawling Chinese script?" Sarah asked, peeking over Ethan's shoulder at the map. It was filled with elaborately drawn paths and arrows. "I studied Ancient Chinese when I was younger... and I happen to have a keen sense of direction," he replied.

"This is coming from the guy who accidentally stumbled upon a Chronos Resurgence device," she snorted.

As they approached yet another hidden entrance, a subtle distortion in the air caught their attention. An ephemeral glow, like a beckoning ember, led them deeper into the sanctuary. The hidden path seemed to unfold before them, an invitation written in the language of ancient secrets.

The sanctuary, bathed in the soft glow of twilight, revealed itself as a garden of blossoms. Lanterns hung from ornate branches, casting a warm luminosity that danced with the fluttering of unseen spirits. Stone pathways meandered through carefully manicured landscapes, leading to a central pavilion where Zin Xia was rumored to await.

As Ethan and Sarah pressed forward, the enticing melody of a guqin resonated through the air, drawing them closer to the heart of the space. The scent of blooming flowers intensified, creating an intoxicating fragrance that seemed to wrap around them like a comforting embrace. Arriving at the pavilion, they were met with a momentary hush—a pause in the rhythmic dance of the guqin. Silence enveloped the sanctuary, and an inexplicable tension hung in the air. The distant echoes of footsteps, too deliberate to belong to the wind, played in their ears. It was then that the subtle glow surrounding them intensified, revealing miniature symbols etched into the stone floor of the pavilion.

In a display of shifting colors, the symbols pulsed with a latent energy. They turned to say something to one another, and just then, the guqin resumed its melody, and the symbols on the ground erupted in a burst of luminescence. An unseen force propelled them into the center of the pavilion, and the air crackled with an electric charge. In an instant, the sanctuary transformed, and the surroundings shifted, revealing towering archways as the music reached a crescendo. When the final notes of the guqin faded away, the realization struck—they had been lured into a trap. Zin Xia was nowhere to be seen. Instead, the area echoed with the presence of unseen observers as the symbols began pulsating at a blinding speed.

Ethan and Sarah found themselves encircled by figures emerging from the shadows—silhouettes clad in robes that seemed to ripple with the essence of temporal energies. The trap had been set, and the Temporal Renegades, masters of manipulation, revealed themselves with an air of triumph.

Amidst the looming shadows of the sanctuary, Sarah swiftly activated her communicator with a sleight of hand, setting off an alarm that urgently called for reinforcements from the Temporal Defense Corps (TDC). She did it so quickly that even Ethan seemed to miss her movements. Both of them reached slowly for their laser, careful not to make a rash move. The figures drew closer and closer as Sarah raked her brain about a plan to stall for time.

Without thinking, she let off a charged attack towards one of the archways that began to crumble a bit but nothing more. She swore under her breath and pressed the alarm signal again, silently praying the Renegades would wait to launch an attack. Not a moment later, a bead of sweat trickled down Sarah's forehead before she exhaled with relief as, one by one, TDC agents materialized in the temporal sanctuary. Her alarm had been received. The reinforcements emerged armed with HEL Pistols and wielding the precision of those trained to navigate the currents of time. The Temporal Renegades, undeterred by the sudden influx of TDC agents, revealed themselves from the veiled periphery. They were draped in attire that seemed to defy the conventions of any specific era and exuded an aura of defiance against the order of the TDC.

The battleground was set, and the clash between the guardians of time and those who sought to disrupt its flow commenced. The HEL Pistols hummed with energy as the two factions converged; the sanctuary transformed into an arena where the very essence of temporal energy crackled like lightning. The battle unfolded with a choreography of precision and chaos. TDC agents, seasoned in the art of temporal combat, engaged the Renegades while beams of disruptive energy streaked through the air, creating vibrant trails of light.

However, despite the TDC's disciplined efforts, the Temporal Renegades displayed a mastery of unpredictability. Their tactics seemed to defy conventional understanding, and the tide of the battle shifted with an unsettling fluidity. The Renegades, guided by an agenda hidden within the folds of time, exhibited a resilience that implied a deeper understanding of the temporal fabric.

As the conflict intensified, the TDC found themselves pushed to the brink. With an uncanny ability to exploit temporal anomalies, the renegades countered the disciplined maneuvers of the guardians of time. The TDC found themselves in a precarious position. They were losing agents, falling behind in hand-to-hand combat, and seemed to be greatly outnumbered. Sarah realizes all is lost; more than half her team has fallen around her, their cries lost over the deafening sounds of death. She knows she must retreat before it is too late.

Chapter 7: To Where Time Takes Us

Just when all hope was lost, a blazing light appeared out of nowhere, causing everyone to be momentarily blinded. Through this light, a white horse broke through with Zin Xia on its back, sword raised, and through her lips escaped a battle cry. She was adorned in armor that gleamed as her blade seemed to capture the essence of time itself, its edge sharp enough to cut through the temporal distortions that pervaded the battlefield.

She took down six Renegade members in one blow. That's when it hit Sarah, Ethan, and the rest of the TDC. She was on their side, and the very air resonated with a newfound sense of hope. The Temporal Renegades, momentarily unsettled by the unexpected turn of events, sought to regroup and confront the new challenge that stood before them. Zin Xia, her steed poised with grace and power, directed her sword toward the heart of the renegade forces. The battle resumed with an intensity that surpassed the earlier tumult. Zin Xia, the beacon of hope, became a tempest on the battlefield, her every movement a harmonious dance with the temporal energies at play.

The sword cleaved through the renegades with a precision that defied the chaotic nature of the conflict. Her steed moved with a grace that defied the limitations of earthly physics, carrying its rider through the clamor with lightning-quick swiftness. The renegades, initially confident in their mastery of temporal manipulation, now faced an adversary whose connection to time transcended their understanding. The sanctuary, once a battleground fraught with uncertainty, now witnessed a transformation. Zin Xia, surrounded by the energies of time, became a force that guided the TDC agents to victory. The few scattered Renegades tried to retreat, but she managed to slay every last one of them, as was her way. There were no survivors.

"We must return to HQ before we disrupt the time continuum any further," Sarah urged before any of them had a chance even to regain their breath. Covered in blood, they made their way through the portal Sarah had opened. Zin Xia dismounted her steed, kissed it on the forehead, and murmured something to it before making her way through the portal as well.

The echoes of battle still reverberated through the sanctuary as the Temporal Defense Corps (TDC) agents materialized in headquarters. A solemn air accompanied the journey back, the TDC agents reflecting on the surreal turn of events that had unfolded on the battleground. Exhaustion had completely taken over each of their battered bodies. The TDC agents who were present at HQ, their expressions a blend of awe and gratitude, gathered around Zin Xia, whose presence had turned the tide of battle. Ethan, his voice laced with admiration, broke the silence that lingered in the aftermath of the clash.

"You saved us back there. We owe you our victory."

Zin Xia, her armor bearing the marks of the recent battle, offered a nod of acknowledgment. "The battle was won not by one, but by the unity of those who safeguard time. It was your resilience that triumphed in the end."

"But why did you wait until now to reveal yourself? We could have used your help sooner." Said Sarah, wiping her face with a towel in an attempt to take off some of the blood that was staining it. A contemplative pause enveloped Zin Xia before she began to speak, her words carrying the weight of centuries.

"I was among you all along, but I chose to weave myself into the fabric of the Temporal Renegades. It was the only way to dismantle them from within, to understand their motivations and tactics intimately."

The TDC agents exchanged glances, absorbing the revelation,

"Why put yourself through such a risk? Why not reveal your allegiance sooner?" Sarah pressed on.

Zin Xia's eyes looked past her and met Ethan's gaze instead. "The Renegades thrive on secrecy and manipulation. I had to play the role convincingly, allowing their overconfidence to be their downfall. Had I revealed myself earlier, the delicate dance of time would have shifted, and our victory might have remained elusive."

"But you erased yourself from history. How could you bear to do that?" Ethan asked, his voice betraying the emotion he was feeling within. A wistful smile played on Zin Xia's lips.

"Every choice has a cost. I erased myself to protect the timeline but left traces—a trail of breadcrumbs. I believed that someone from the TDC would eventually discover these remnants and unravel the truth. I chose to fade into shadows of time, leaving behind subtle imprints for those keen enough to perceive them."

"You risked everything for us, for the timeline. We owe you more than words can express."

"I need to know more, though," Sarah interjected in her usual determined manner, and Ethan was sure he could sense the challenging tone she had taken on. He understood why she was suspicious but could not begin to believe that Zin Xia was anything more than a savior. Seated in a room adorned with holographic displays depicting temporal anomalies, Zin Xia began to share the intricacies of her mission.

"The Renegades sought to exploit temporal disruptions for their own agenda. By integrating myself into their ranks, I gained insights into their plans and discovered vulnerabilities that we could exploit."

A holographic representation unfolded before them, showcasing Zin Xia's interactions with the Renegades. Dialogues, strategic maneuvers, and moments of peril illuminated the room, revealing the hidden layers of her mission.

"As I delved deeper into their ranks," Zin Xia continued, "I realized the extent of their influence across various eras. Their manipulation of key events threatened to destabilize the very foundations of time. It was a battle not only against their forces but against the distortions they sought to introduce into history."

Ethan, absorbing the holographic narrative, asked, "Did you always know you would succeed?"

Zin Xia's response carried a serene certainty. "The threads of time are unpredictable, but unity and determination can bend them in our favor. I had faith in the strength of the TDC and believed that, with the right guidance, you would overcome the challenges presented by the Renegades."

The holographic display shifted to reveal the moment of Zin Xia's triumphant arrival on the battlefield. The TDC agents who were watching hooted and cheered while Sarah remained silent, a stoic expression on her face. As the holographic display dimmed, the TDC agents found themselves inspired by the sacrifice and strategy they had just witnessed. After the revelations and battles, the Temporal Defense Corps headquarters settled into a contemplative calm.

Ethan, still processing the weight of Zin Xia's sacrifice, approached her with a soft smile. "You have done so much. Is there anything we can do for you?"

"I appreciate your words, but my journey has been one of duty and sacrifice. Now, as the threads of time settle, I must find my place within them."

"How about we start by taking you home? Until you figure out where you belong in time, consider the TDC your temporary anchor." He replied.

"I hardly think that's appropriate." Sarah snorted. "It's fine, Sarah. I think we all need to regroup, and I have the space," Ethan told her.

"Home," Zin Xia echoed, a word laden with both familiarity and a touch of longing. "I appreciate your kindness, Ethan."

They received the necessary approvals from TDC Command and left HQ for his place. As they arrived at Ethan's home, a cozy dwelling with a view of the city's skyline, he extended a welcoming gesture. "Make yourself at home. You're welcome to use that shower in the guest room, and I will leave out some spare clothes for you. After I shower, I'll whip up something to eat. What's your favorite cuisine?"

"At this point, anything except Chinese."

They both laughed and headed separate ways to clean up. When Ethan was done, he left clothes out on the guest room bed and ventured into the kitchen. The aroma of fresh ingredients filled the air as he began to craft a meal inspired by his favorite fusion of flavors. The sizzle of pans and the rhythmic chopping of vegetables provided a comforting soundtrack to the unfolding evening. As Ethan set the table, adorned with an array of dishes, Zin Xia appeared still drying her damp hair.

"This is a feast," she remarked, her eyes sparkling with anticipation.

Ethan, wearing an apron adorned with a Star Wars motif, grinned. "I figured a legendary warrior deserves a legendary meal. Let's start with these spring rolls—they're a mix of earthy vegetables and a hint of exotic spices."

They engaged in light banter, the conversation weaving between tales of Zin Xia's ancient adventures and Ethan's affinity for science fiction. The main course arrived, a symphony of flavors comprising a delicate balance of textures and tastes. Ethan explained each dish with infectious enthusiasm.

"Here we have a fusion of Asian and Mediterranean influences. The sweet and tangy teriyaki-glazed salmon complements the zesty couscous salad perfectly."

"This is excellent," she remarked, savoring the hot food.

As the meal progressed, the conversation took a more personal turn. Zin Xia spoke of her past and the loved ones she had left behind in order to preserve the fabric of time.

"I had a family once," Zin Xia shared, her eyes reflecting a distant memory. "The Renegades preyed on personal attachments, and to protect time, I had to relinquish my own."

"That must have been incredibly difficult. To sacrifice personal happiness for the greater good."

"In safeguarding time, I found solace in the duty I carried. But now and then, the echoes of those lost attachments resonate through the corridors of my memories."

Ethan, compelled by a genuine connection, offered a comforting presence. "Sometimes, the threads of the heart are as intricate as those of time. I can't fathom the sacrifices you've made, but I'm grateful for what you've done for us."

As they lingered over dessert, a decadent fusion of chocolate and fruits, Ethan couldn't help but express his sentiments. "Zin Xia, there's something about you—a presence that transcends time. I feel a connection that goes beyond the battle we've faced."

"Time has a way of weaving unexpected bonds. Perhaps our threads are entwined for reasons beyond our understanding."

"I never expected my love for science fiction and exploration to lead to this—a connection that feels both ancient and new." He got up and led her to the balcony overlooking the cityscape. Zin Xia looked out in amazement toward the cityscape, " beautiful and yet so busy." As she turned toward Ethan, he took a step closer to her, and she hesitated for a moment before gently reaching for her hand. Their fingers intertwined, bridging the space between them before he pulled her closer still and kissed her.

Chapter 8: Looping Through the Timeline

Zin Xia spent the next several weeks outlining the Temporal Renegades' goals and training their methods to the guardians of time, TDC agents. During one of her briefings at the end, Director Williams approached Zin Xia, How would you like to join our ranks as one of us? he inquired. Zin Xia said, "I accept with honor." Good Director Williams said, "I took a chance to see if you would agree." The event is set for tomorrow; as they say, time waits for no one.

The air was charged with a sense of reverence, acknowledging the legendary warrior's pivotal role in safeguarding time. Ethan was dressed in formal attire, befitting the occasion, and stood alongside Sarah as they welcomed Zin Xia to the heart of the TDC. The ceremony took place in a state-of-the-art chamber adorned with holographic displays that depicted the pivotal moments in time charged with temporal energies. Director Williams, a figure of authority within the TDC, began the proceedings with a solemn address.

"Today, we stand witness to a convergence of past and present—a moment where a legendary warrior, Zin Xia, becomes an integral part of the Temporal Defense Corps. Her sacrifices and unwavering commitment to the timeline have earned her a place among us."

Zin Xia, wearing ceremonial armor that reflected the essence of her ancient legacy, stood with quiet grace. The TDC agents in attendance, their respect evident, awaited the formalities the same way they had when Ethan and his peers were inducted.

"Zin Xia, your journey has been one of valor and duty. Today, we extend our hand in unity, welcoming you into the fold of those who stand as guardians of time."

As Director Williams concluded his address, Ethan stepped forward, holding a symbolic artifact—a representation of unity and shared purpose within the TDC.

"On behalf of the Temporal Defense Corps, I present you with this emblem. May it serve as a reminder of the bonds we share and the duty we uphold together."

Zin Xia accepted the emblem with a respectful nod, her eyes reflecting gratitude.

"I am honored to stand among you, guardians of time."

As the ceremony came to a close, there was a round of applause. The holographic displays dimmed, leaving the chamber bathed in soft light as the TDC agents dispersed. Zin Xia, now officially a member of the Temporal Defense Corps, moved seamlessly among her new allies, ready to embark on the challenges that awaited them in the ever-shifting currents of time.

Three days after her official induction into the Temporal Defense Corps (TDC), Ethan and Zin Xia found themselves in the holographic briefing room. Director Williams, or rather the projection of him, addressed them with a sense of urgency.

"Agents, the Renegades have disrupted the Indus Valley Civilization timeline. Anachronistic elements have surfaced, threatening the delicate balance of this ancient civilization. It's imperative that you address this anomaly and restore the historical integrity of the Indus Valley."

Ethan, leaning against a holographic display table, exchanged a glance with Zin Xia. "Indus Valley, huh? I've always been a fan of ancient civilizations. This should be interesting."

Zin Xia, her gaze met Ethans. "Let's ensure we leave no stone unturned, both literally and figuratively."

As they activated the Chronos Resurgence, the holographic landscape shifted, transporting them to the banks of the mighty Indus River during the height of ancient civilization. The air carried the scent of fertile soil, and the distant hum of city life echoed through the valley. Their mission became apparent as they strolled through the bustling streets of Mohenjo-Daro, the city revealing itself in meticulous detail. The Indus Valley denizens moved with purpose, engaging in trade, craftsmanship, and communal activities that defined the civilization's prosperity. Ethan, noticing anachronistic disruptions, pointed toward a marketplace where unusual artifacts were being traded. "Looks like the Renegades brought some futuristic tech to the ancient world. That's not going to go unnoticed."

"Let's investigate discreetly. We need to identify the source of these disturbances and neutralize them without altering the course of history."

Amidst the historic structures and bustling marketplaces, they discovered a hidden chamber where Renegade agents had set up a temporal disruptor. This device, blending futuristic technology with the ancient surroundings, was responsible for the disruptions that threatened the timeline. Eyeing the disruptor with a mix of fascination and concern, Ethan quipped, "Talk about bringing a sledgehammer to a ceramics class. These Renegades sure know how to make an entrance."

The duo engaged in a coordinated effort to dismantle the temporal disruptor, their movements a combination of precision and skill. As the disruptor's core deactivated, the surroundings vibrated with a momentary distortion before settling into a restored harmony.

"The Indus Valley has been safeguarded. Let's ensure that the historical framework remains unmarred and take this back with us for Command to take a look at," Zin Xia responded, pointing at the equipment they had just deactivated.

"Teamwork makes the timeline work, right?" Ethan laughed, impressed by the seamless collaboration as they gathered the pieces.

When they activated the Chronos Resurgence to return to TDC headquarters, the comforting smell of the warm land was replaced with the crispy clinical scent of their own time.

"It seems that the Indus Valley was just a clever rouse to throw us off track. Their real target is the Renaissance period." Sarah's voice cut through the sound of them piecing together the disrupter.

"Oh, hi there. The Renaissance, you say? I'm down for a little back-to-back time leap," Ethan responded as he turned to see her entering through the automatic doors.

"Sure, me too. Sounds like fun," Zin Xia grinned as Sarah led them to re-suit up.

In the depths of the Renaissance, amidst the endless avenues of art, culture, and intellectual fervor, Ethan, Zin Xia, and Sarah found themselves on a mission to rectify the real disruptions caused by the Renegades. The Chronos Resurgence transported them to Florence, Italy, the epicenter of that time. The trio emerged in the midst of the bustling Piazza della Signoria, surrounded by architectural marvels and the symphony of creativity that defined the era. The air carried the scent of parchment, ink, and the whispers of artists shaping history.

"Talk about a time machine's greatest hits playlist. Renaissance Florence, the birthplace of the artistic revolution!" Ethan squealed with a grin that made him look ten years younger.

"Our task is to ensure that this revolution unfolds without interference. Let's explore discreetly and identify any disturbances." Sarah chided but couldn't help but smile at his infectious eagerness.

As they strolled through the streets, witnessing the awe-inspiring works of Leonardo da Vinci, Michelangelo, and other luminaries, Sarah noted,

"The Renegades have left their mark here. We need to locate the source of disruption and neutralize it."

Their journey led them to the workshop of a renowned artist, where anachronistic tools and materials hinted at the intrusion of future tech, which would cause far more ripples than what they had done in the Indus Valley Civilization. This would alter history on too many levels for even the TDC to fix if they had discovered it any later.

"Renegade Agents. Take cover," Sarah barked as the three of them managed to dodge a hailstorm of laser shots that came from the side. A confrontation ensued as Renegade agents, clad in attire that clashed with the Renaissance aesthetic, attempted to defend their temporal disruptor.

"Don't let them escape," Sarah pressed on as she shot back, directly stunning one renegade who fell to the ground.

Zin Xia, displaying expert marksmanship with a temporal disruptor neutralizer, joined the fray. "Ethan, Sarah, cover me! I'm going for the disruptor."

Ethan, with a flourish of his holographic rapier, bantered, "On it!" and took the second one down. Only one Renegade was left. As Zin Xia skillfully disabled the temporal disruptor, the Renegade, recognizing the inevitability of defeat, retreated with a temporal flash. The disruption that had threatened the Renaissance's historical fabric dissipated, leaving behind a city restored to its creative zenith.

"Two for two. Not bad, eh?" Ethan asked as Sarah started gathering the pieces of the disrupter.

"I got to say, this is pretty insane," Zin Xia sheepishly admitted as she helped Sarah. As they prepared to return to the present, the Chronos Resurgence activated, enveloping them in a temporal field. Back in the TDC headquarters, Director Williams acknowledged their success.

"Agents, your dedication to preserving the threads of time is commendable. The Renaissance stands unblemished thanks to your intervention."

After a successful mission preserving the Renaissance, Ethan and Zin Xia found themselves back at Ethan's apartment. The city lights outside cast a gentle glow into the living space, creating an ambiance of comfort and familiarity. Zin Xia, her armor now replaced by more casual attire, moved with graceful ease as she prepared to share a piece of her past with them. In the kitchen, the tantalizing aroma of authentic Chinese cuisine filled the air.

"You know, if saving timelines and being a martial arts master are prerequisites for a dinner date, consider me sold."

Zin Xia, her laughter echoing through the apartment, replied, "Consider it a perk of the job. Now, can you lay the table? Dinner will be served shortly."

As they sat at the dining table, the spread before them an array of delectable dishes, Zin Xia began to share a piece of her personal history. "Growing up, my father was my mentor in martial arts. He believed in training me as fiercely as he trained the boys in our village. It was his way of ensuring I could face any challenge life threw my way."

"Sounds like a remarkable man. I bet the boys had a hard time keeping up with you."

Zin Xia's eyes held a twinkle of nostalgia. "Indeed, they did. My father saw no distinction between us when it came to honing martial skills. It instilled in me a deep sense of gratitude and resilience."

As they savored the flavors of ancient Chinese cuisine, Zin Xia continued her tale. "There were days when the training seemed relentless, but my father's lessons went beyond physical prowess. He taught me discipline, perseverance, and the strength that comes from embracing challenges head-on."

Ethan, through a mouthful of the sumptuous feast, wondered, "Your father sounds like he knew the secret to raising a warrior. I can see where you get your strength and grace from."

Her expression softened, a blend of appreciation and affection. "His guidance shaped the person I am today. I carry his teachings with me, not just in martial arts but in every aspect of my journey through time."

As the evening unfolded, the conversation flowed seamlessly between stories of ancient traditions, shared laughter, and the unspoken connection that bound them. The city lights outside painted a tableau of warmth and companionship.

"I feel like I've known you for more than just the moments we've spent together. There's a depth to you that transcends time." He said solemnly.

Zin Xia's eyes, meeting Ethan's, acknowledged the shared resonance that echoed through their experiences as she wrapped her arms around Ethan's neck, "I agree, but if I have learned anything, it is that time can take away anything. And yet, it heals all wounds."

Chapter 9: Temporal Symphony in Zrerphis

After their cozy dinner, the following day, they went on another mission using the time-travel device Chronos Resurgence. This time, they arrived at a city named Zrerphis. The city looked like a mix of the coolest sci-fi movies and a history museum. The Chronos Resurgence hummed with energy as it transported Ethan, Zin Xia, and Sarah to Zrerphis, a city that existed at the nexus of time, where the past and future meld in a breathtaking display of architectural marvels. The trio found themselves standing on a platform overlooking a metropolis that defied common notions of urban landscapes. Towers of sleek, reflective surfaces intertwined with structures similar to ancient civilizations create a seamless blend of futuristic innovation and historical homage.

Ethan gaped in awe, his eyes tracing the contours of skyscrapers adorned with holographic projections of ancient eras. "Well, this is a city planner's dream come true. I've seen glimpses of the future, but this... this is something else!"

Zin Xia, with her sharp eyes, noticed that Zrerphis existed at the crossroads of time. She thought the Renegades were up to no good, messing with time for their own reasons."Zrerphis appears to be a convergence point for various timelines. The Renegades must be exploiting this temporal crossroads for their own ends."

As they descended into the heart of the city, they stared at the coexistence of sleek hovercraft weaving between ancient-style market stalls, where holographic merchants peddled wares that spanned centuries. The air resonated with a harmony of temporal echoes, each note representing a distinct era that contributed to the city's unique music.

Sarah, ever the pragmatist, remarked, "I've seen my fair share of strange cities, but this one takes the cake. How are we supposed to pinpoint the disruptions in this temporal maze?"

Zin Xia replied with sharp focus, "We'll need to attune ourselves to the subtle anomalies. The Renegades may have left traces that disrupt the natural flow of time."

All of them navigated through bustling streets where citizens, dressed in attire spanning centuries, went about their daily lives. Temporal distortions became evident as they encountered bags of reality where time seemed to warp, creating visual glitches in the routes of the city.

Sitting at a holographic display flickering with revival-era art, Ethan mused, "It's like a historical kaleidoscope. But I guess not all disruptions are as visually appealing."

Their journey led them to the heart of Zrerphis, a central plaza where a colossal temporal disruptor stood, emanating pulses of energy that reverberated through the city. The disruptor, a fusion of futuristic technology and ancient symbols, seemed to draw power from the temporal crossroads surrounding Zrerphis.

"This disruptor is siphoning temporal energy from multiple eras," Zin Xia observed, her eyes narrowing with determination. "We need to disable it before the distortions cascade further."

As they approached the disruptor, Renegade agents appeared, clad in suits that mirrored the eclectic blend of the city itself. A confrontation opened, blaster shots colliding with holographic shields and resonating clashes of temporal disruptors.

Ethan, wielding a holographic shield and deflecting shots with practiced finesse, called out, "Zin Xia, any suggestions on a plan of attack?"

Gracefully evading attacks with martial skills, Zin Xia replied, "We need to disrupt the troublemaker. Sarah, cover us while Ethan and I target the core."

With strategic precision, the three coordinated their efforts. Zin Xia engaged the Renegade agents in close combat, creating openings for Ethan to approach the disruptor's core. Sarah, perched on a vantage point, provided cover fire, ensuring the Renegades couldn't regroup.

As Ethan reached the core, he noted intricate symbols pulsating with temporal energy. With a swift motion, he deactivated the disruptor's core, sending ripples of temporal correction through the city. The Renegade agents, foil in their attempt to manipulate time, retreated with a flash, leaving Zrerphis bathed in the serene glow of restored temporal echoes.

The city, once a canvas of temporal disruptions, settled into a peaceful melody. The citizens of Zrerphis, oblivious to the covert battle fought in their nub, continued their lives in a seamless blend of past, present, and future.

Back at TDC headquarters, Director Williams commended the team for their success in Zrerphis. "Agents, your adaptability in navigating the complexities of Zrerphis is commendable. You've preserved a city that exists at the crossroads of time."

As the holographic displays dimmed, Ethan turned to Zin Xia and Sarah, a successful grin on her face. "Well, that was a rollercoaster. Who knew saving a city could be so... temporally challenging?"

Zin Xia, a glint of amusement in her eyes, replied, "In our line of work, every mission is a journey through the currents of time. We adapt and overcome."

They, united by shared victories and the friendship formed in the crucible of temporal battles, prepared for the next chapter in their ongoing mission to safeguard time. As they moved into the unknown, the echoes of Zrerphis hung—a testament to the strength of a city that defied the constraints of a linear timeline.

The other day, the Temporal Defense Corps (TDC) received a message about a big problem. There was someone causing chaos in the timeline, and they called this person The Anachronist. This troublemaker had the power to mess up time in a huge way.

TDC sent the message to Ethan, Zin Xia, and Sarah, assigning them the mission to deal with The Anachronist. As they got the order, Zin Xia, Ethan, and Sarah geared up for a tough mission. The Anachronist was no ordinary adversary. They found themselves in a desolate landscape, a place outside the regular flow of time. Ethan stared around, murmuring with a smirk, "This would be interesting; I can't wait for this one."

Suddenly, The Anachronist appeared, surrounded by swirling temporal distortions. The air crackled with energy, and the team knew they were in for a tough fight. The Anachronist spoke in a haunting voice, "Time is my canvas, and I'll paint it however I please."

The battle began, and The Anachronist opened waves of temporal disruptions as Renegades appeared through the waves. Ethan, Sarah, and Zin Xia fought with everything they had, but The Anachronist seemed to be one step ahead, bending time to their will.

Between the chaos, Zin Xia closed her eyes for a moment. When she opened them, a spectral version of herself appeared beside her. This presence had a calm aura, and it seemed to resonate with the time.

Zin Xia's spectral form moved with grace, countering The Anachronist's. It was like a dance, a dance between the chaos of The Anachronist and the harmony of Zin Xia's spectral presence.

Ethan and Sarah, seeing this unique collaboration, felt a surge of hope. Zin Xia's spectral form became a stable point in the time storm. The team rallied around her, finding strength in the balance she brought to the fight.

The battle continued, but with Zin Xia's spectral presence, the team gained ground. The Anachronist, realizing they couldn't play with time as freely with Zin Xia around, got frustrated.

Ethan, using his holographic shield, shouted, "Zin Xia, you're the key! Keep it up!"

Zin Xia, both her physical and spectral forms in sync, nodded. "We need to disrupt The Anachronist's hold on time. Together, we can bring stability."

The team worked together, combining their skills to counter The Anachronists. Zin Xia's spectral presence acted like an anchor, keeping the time disturbances in check.

With a final coordinated effort, they managed to weaken The Anachronist's control over time. The Anachronists and the remaining few Renegades, realizing they were losing, vanished with a burst of temporal energy.

The city, once in the grip of time chaos, started to settle. Zin Xia's spectral form faded away, and the team found themselves back in regular time.

Director Williams, through the holographic communicator, praised the team, "You did it! The Anachronist's plan is foiled. Time is back on track."

Ethan, catching his breath, grinned at Zin Xia, "You're not just a master of martial arts, but a timekeeper too!"

With a hint of a smile, Zin Xia replied, "In the dance of time, we all play our part. Let's be ready for whatever comes next."

As the team prepared for the next mission, Ethan couldn't help but think about the layers he was uncovering in Zin Xia's character. He found her practicing martial arts in a quiet corner of the training area.

"Zin Xia, mind showing me some of those moves? I feel like there's a lot more to your story than we know," Ethan asked, genuine curiosity in his voice.

Zin Xia nodded, and they engaged in a brief brawling session. Ethan, despite his best efforts, struggled to match Zin Xia's fluid movements.

"You fight well, Ethan. But there's a depth to martial arts that goes beyond physical skill. It's about understanding the universe," Zin Xia explained.

Their conversation continued as they shared a quiet moment in the training area. Zin Xia spoke of her ancient origins, the traditions passed down through generations, and the duty she felt to protect time.

Ethan, listening intently, realized that Zin Xia's journey wasn't just about battling Renegades and fixing troubles. It was a personal quest intertwined with a legacy that stretched across centuries.

Later, during a mission in a medieval kingdom, Zin Xia's air shifted as she expertly navigated the customs and protocols of the time. Ethan, witnessing her adaptability, remarked, "You're like a time traveler and a cultural chameleon all in one."

Zin Xia smiled, "In my time, adaptability is a necessity. It's not just about preserving history; it's about understanding the variation that makes each era unique."

In ancient civilizations, Zin Xia embraced the role of a wise mentor, guiding communities through challenges. In futuristic landscapes, she demonstrated a keen understanding of technology, seamlessly blending tradition with innovation.

During a mission set in a cyberpunk future, where neon lights clashed with ancient architecture, Ethan found himself marveling at Zin Xia's adaptability. "You're like a time-traveling chameleon, Zin Xia. Whether its ancient kingdoms or futuristic landscapes, you navigate with grace."

Zin Xia, her eyes reflecting a blend of ancient wisdom and contemporary insight, replied with a touch of humor, "Well, adapting to different eras keeps life interesting. Besides, a warrior's got to stay versatile."

Their banter, a mixture of admiration and playful bond, became a hallmark of their missions. In a medieval setting, Ethan found himself surrounded by knights in shining armor. Zin Xia, with a wry smile, teased, "Thinking of upgrading your wardrobe, Ethan? Shiny armor has a certain charm, doesn't it?"

Ethan, pretending to inspect his holographic attire, replied with a grin, "I don't know. I think I'll stick to the holographic look. It's more... futuristic."

As they faced The Anachronist in a tumultuous temporal landscape, Ethan couldn't help but acknowledge the depth of his respect for Zin Xia. "You're not just a warrior, Zin Xia. You're a force that transcends time. I've seen you face challenges with a strength that goes beyond any era's definition."

Zin Xia, touched by his words, responded with sincerity, "In the laps of time, we find paths of connection. I'm grateful for the bond we share, Ethan."

Fthan's admiration for Zin Xia evolved into a profound respect, creating a bond that transcended the boundaries of time.

The challenges of navigating through time, a profound and undeniable love began to blossom within Ethan's heart. It wasn't just a fleeting emotion; it became a driving force in his dedication to the Temporal Defense Corps.

One evening, after a particularly intense mission, Ethan and Zin Xia found themselves on a rooftop overlooking a city from a bygone era. The moon hung in the sky, casting a gentle glow over the ancient architecture.

Ethan, looking at Zin Xia with warmth in his eyes, couldn't help but express the feelings that had been growing within him. "Zin Xia, in this time, you've become a constant path, weaving through my every moment. It's more than admiration—it's love."

Zin Xia, her gaze meeting his, felt a tender resonance. "Ethan, time has taught me the value of connections that transcend the ages. Your love is a gift that spans the eras, and I cherish it."

The city around them seemed to fade as Ethan took a step closer to Zin Xia. In that timeless moment, he gently held her hand, and they stood together, immersed in the quiet beauty of their shared emotions.

"Ethan," Zin Xia whispered, "our journey through time has been filled with challenges, but your love has been a constant, grounding force. It gives me strength beyond the battles we face."

Ethan, his voice filled with sincerity, replied, "Zin Xia, you're not just a warrior in the pages of history. You're the beating heart of my present, my past, and the future we'll shape together."

The moonlit rooftop became a stage for their shared affection, and in that quiet space, Ethan and Zin Xia found solace in each other's presence. Their love became a source of inspiration, a driving force that fueled their dedication to the Temporal Defense Corps.

As they embraced the depth of their connection, Ethan knew that no matter the challenges time threw their way, their love would endure, a constant in the ever-changing currents of the timeline.

In the quiet moments after their moonlit embrace, Ethan couldn't shake the nagging question that lingered in his mind. As the love between him and Zin Xia deepened, so did his urge to uncover the truth behind her mysterious disappearance from historical records.

Night swallowed Ethan after their long journey. Zin Xia watched him sleep and whispered, "Gotta go, Ethan. Hope my message wakes you." Then, she stood close, feeling his warmth. A sad smile kissed her lips. Tiptoeing, she left, his love a bittersweet ache in her heart.

Sunlight kissed Ethan's face, stirring him awake. His heart sank to see Zin Xia gone. "Zin Xia?" he called, voice cracking. Panic bubbled as only silence answered.

Suddenly, a flash of red drew his eye. On the corner of the roof lay a dusty box, a single button screaming for attention. "PUSH," it demanded, with an arrow pointing at the bright red danger.

Footsteps approached, and the door slammed to the wall. Sarah came racing towards him, her face etched with worry. "Ethan? What's wrong?"

Ethan pointed at the box, his voice shaky. "Zin Xia... gone. This box... 'Push,' it says." As Ethan pushed the button, a holographic message unexpectedly flickered to life before them. Zin Xia's voice echoed in Ethan's ears, her words carrying a weight that stirred both concern and determination.

"Ethan, your path is intertwined with mine," her voice resonated through the air. "There is a darkness that seeks to erase me from history. You are the key to our salvation."

As the echoes of Zin Xia's holographic message lingered in the air, Ethan felt a profound sense of purpose. The mystery of her potential erasure from history had added a new layer to their already complex journey through time. With each step, the weight of responsibility grew on Ethan's shoulders, but so did his determination.

Back at TDC headquarters, Ethan sought guidance from Director Williams. The holographic displays flickered to life, and the trio, joined by the Director, gathered for a discussion.

"Ethan," Director Williams began, "Zin Xia's message indicates a threat that transcends mere temporal disruptions. It's as if the fabric of history itself is at risk. Unraveling this mystery will require caution and strategic thinking."

Ethan nodded, his determination unwavering. "Director Zin Xia is not just a partner in missions; she's become an integral part of my journey. I won't rest until we uncover the truth and ensure she remains a constant in the pages of history."

Sarah, her pragmatic voice cutting through the air, added, "We've faced tough challenges before, but this one feels different. The Renegades might be meddling with something far more consequential than we've encountered."

Zin Xia, her presence felt even in her absence, became the focal point of their discussion. Director Williams, acknowledging the significance of their mission, emphasized, "The impact of Zin Xia's holographic message is undeniable. We must proceed with caution, gather intel, and understand the nature of this threat before taking any decisive actions."

The holographic displays projected images of historical records, timelines, and fragments of Zin Xia's journey through time. Ethan, fueled by a mixture of love and determination, delved into the research, seeking clues that could unravel the mystery.

As the team prepared for the next phase of their mission, Ethan couldn't help but reflect on the profound impact Zin Xia had on him. Her disappearance from historical records wasn't just a threat to the fabric of time; it was a personal challenge that fueled his determination to redefine the course of their shared narrative.

Chapter 10: Unraveling Threads

The lingering image of Zin Xia's spectral form flickered in Ethan's mind, her final message resonating with a profound urgency. He knew, with an unwavering certainty, that her disappearance wasn't a mere anomaly. It was a thread leading to a deeper truth, a truth he was determined to unravel.

His next destination now was an era shrouded in the mists of time, a place where towering castles kissed the clouds and magic flowed with the wind. This wasn't just any historical period; it was a time adorned with kingdoms and mysticism, a stage where the truth about Zin Xia's past might resonate the strongest.

He knew he wouldn't be making this perilous journey alone. Sarah, her eyes mirroring his unwavering resolve, stood beside him. Her presence, a constant reminder of their shared bond with Zin Xia, bolstered his spirit. They were a team once more, united by a purpose that transcended personal loss.

The absence of Zin Xia, however, cast a long shadow. Her combat prowess, her tactical brilliance, and her unwavering loyalty were irreplaceable. Ethan knew this journey would be fraught with danger, each step a gamble without the shield of her expertise. Yet, the void she left was a constant motivator, a burning ember fueling his determination.

He was venturing into the past, not just for himself but for Zin Xia's sake. Her sacrifice deserved answers and her disappearance demanded a resolution. This journey was a pilgrimage, a quest to honor her memory and uncover the secrets she held close.

With a deep breath, Ethan and Sarah gripped the Chronos Resurgence. A blinding flash of light engulfed them, momentarily erasing the familiar surroundings of the TDC headquarters. When their vision cleared, the world around them had transformed. The landscape was dominated by towering castles, whose spires reached the clouds, whispering tales of lost battles and magical secrets with their imposing silhouettes. Their faces were touched by a cool breeze that smelled of freshly baked bread and woodsmoke.

The air itself had a unique quality, possessing a familiar yet foreign energy. Ethan and Sarah exchanged a nervous glance, a mixture of anxiety and exhilaration bubbling within them. This was it. The ancient era, a realm shrouded in the mists of time, lay before them. Each step they took would be a leap into the unknown, a journey fraught with peril. They had no idea what dangers lurked around the corner, what secrets the past held, or what challenges they would face.

"Let's explore this place first," Ethan said to Sarah.

Sarah placed a hand on his arm. "Alright," she responded, her voice laced with concern, "but we have to be careful, Ethan. We don't know what kind of dangers this era holds."

Ethan squeezed her hand reassuringly. "I know, Sarah. But remember, Zin Xia's message led us here. We have to find out what happened to her."

"And what if it's a trap?" Sarah countered, her gaze sweeping across the bustling marketplace. "What if someone here knows about the Chronos Resurgence, about our abilities?"

Ethan met her worried eyes. "We'll be cautious. We'll blend in, gather information, and only reveal ourselves when absolutely necessary."

He paused, a thoughtful expression crossing his face. "Besides, we're not alone in this. Zin Xia's spirit is with us, guiding us."

Sarah offered a weak smile. "I know, but that doesn't mean I won't worry sick about you every step of the way."

Ethan chuckled, the sound warm and genuine. "I appreciate that, Sarah. But trust me, I'll be careful. We both need to get out of this alive."

They continued their walk through the crowded streets. Navigating the bustling cityscape was a sensory overload. Ethan and Sarah weaved through throngs of people, their modern attire drawing curious glances. As they left the city walls behind, the landscape transformed. Rolling hills, dotted with grazing sheep and quaint villages, stretched towards a majestic mountain range shrouded in mist. The air grew cooler, carrying the scent of pine and damp earth.

Finally, they reached a narrow, overgrown path leading into the mountainside. The entrance to an ancient cave, barely visible beneath a curtain of vines, gaped before them.

Ethan turned to Sarah, his gaze resolute. "This is it. I'll go in and see what I can find. Stay here, keep watch."

Sarah placed a hand on his arm, her eyes filled with concern. "Be careful, Ethan. Remember, we don't know what dangers lurk within."

Ethan squeezed her hand reassuringly. "I'll be alright. Zin Xia's message led us here. I have to find out what happened to her."

With a final nod, Ethan shouldered his backpack and vanished into the darkness of the cave. Sarah settled herself near the entrance, her senses on high alert. The only sounds on the mountain were the rustle of leaves in the wind and the scattered chirp of a bird.

Ethan dove into the pitch-black cave, the only sound rising above the deafening silence except for his own ragged breaths. With its familiar, comforting, smooth surface, he fumbled for the holographic device in the darkness. He turned on Zin Xia's hologram, casting a glow that lit up the walls of the cavern.

He could never have imagined the sight that met his eyes. Each elaborate mural that covered the cave walls featured a scene from Zin Xia's life. Here, a young Zin Xia, who was hardly a woman, practiced her warrior techniques with a fierce intensity. There, she stood resolute, the Chronos Resurgence clutched in her hand, a newly appointed guardian entrusted with the protection of the temporal flow.

As Ethan traced the murals with his fingertips, he felt a connection to Zin Xia's past, a shared thread woven through the tapestry of time. He saw her battles fought, her victories celebrated, and the sacrifices she made to safeguard the delicate balance of time.

Scattered amongst the murals were artifacts: a worn leather journal, a dented helmet, and a polished sword that hummed with otherworldly energy. Each item told a story, a fragment of Zin Xia's journey. He picked up the journal, its pages filled with meticulous notes and cryptic symbols. As he deciphered the faded script, a picture emerged of Zin Xia's relentless pursuit of knowledge, her quest to understand the intricacies of temporal manipulation.

As Ethan traced the intricate inscriptions drawn across the cave walls, a revelation dawned upon him. He learned of the Nexus Point, a place that held the temporal balance, a focal point where the very fabric of time converged. It was not any place in the timeline but a realm. Following the inscription, he also learned about the Chronos gate, a hidden gateway woven into the very fabric of time, a secret known only to a select few guardians throughout history. That place, he understood, was the source of the Chronos Resurgence devices' power.

The revelation about the Chronos Resurgence devices struck Ethan like a bolt of lightning. They were far rarer than he ever imagined. There were only a few of them, and he knew that he possessed one, as did Sarah and Zin Xia. But the inscription on the cave wall left a chilling implication hanging in the air.

"If these devices are so scarce," he murmured to himself, his voice echoing in the cavernous silence, "who else might have one?"

The thought sent a shiver down his spine. "If others possessed the Chronos Resurgence, they could be using it for their own purposes. Malicious purposes. The delicate balance of time, the very fabric of reality, could be at stake."

Ethan's heart pounded with a mix of awe. The responsibility shouldered by Zin Xia and the other guardians suddenly seemed immense. They weren't just warriors; they were the gatekeepers of time, the silent guardians ensuring the delicate balance of the universe remained undisturbed.

A cold dread settled in his stomach. The mission had just become exponentially more dangerous. It wasn't just about finding Zin Xia anymore. It was about protecting the very fabric of time from those who might seek to exploit its power for their own gain.

He turned to the faint glow emanating from Zin Xia's hologram, his voice heavy with newfound understanding.

"I never truly grasped the weight you carried, Zin Xia," he confessed, his voice echoing in the cavernous silence. "The burden of protecting the flow of time…it's far greater than I ever imagined. I promise that I will do whatever I can to protect the timeline from anyone who tries to mess with it."

He had to find Zin Xia. He knew the journey ahead would be fraught with danger, but the thought of Zin Xia, her sacrifice, and the responsibility that now fell upon him fueled his determination.

The weight of the revelations pressed down on Ethan like a physical force. The air was heavy and stagnant, and the cave walls seemed to close in. He experienced dizziness and a sick feeling that overwhelmed him. He needed to get away from the claustrophobic atmosphere and get some fresh air.

Following Zin Xia's hologram's dim glow, Ethan went back through the maze-like cavern. He became even more disoriented as the passages appeared to twist and turn in an impossible way. Though panic gnawed at the corners of his consciousness, he forced himself to stay composed. He concentrated on the slight wind, a current of clean air that felt as though it was calling him to the exit.

Finally, after a seemingly endless struggle, a sliver of light appeared in the distance. Hope surged through him as he stumbled towards it, heart pounding in his chest. As he neared the cave's mouth, a bloodcurdling scream shattered the silence. It was Sarah, her voice laced with terror. Panic seized him. He sprinted out of the cave, tripping over loose rock and falling hard on his knees, scraping them raw. Ignoring the pain, he scrambled to his feet, his gaze frantically searching for Sarah.

The sight that greeted him sent a jolt of ice through his veins. Sarah lay sprawled on the ground, her clothes smoldering with faint burn marks. Her chest heaved with ragged breaths, her eyes wide with fear.

"Sarah!" Ethan cried out, rushing to her side. Kneeling beside her, he gripped her shoulders. "Hey, Sarah, what happened?"

She gasped for air, her voice barely a whisper. "Enemies... attack..." she managed to croak, her hand weakly pointing towards the dense undergrowth.

Chapter 11: Echoes of Destiny

Ethan, panicking, swiped at the sweat on his forehead, inadvertently smearing Sarah's blood from his hand across his face. As her breath started weakening, she struggled to keep her eyes open. Composing himself, he told her, "Sarah, stay with me, okay?" Checking for the wound, he pulled up her shirt a little, revealing two gashes with burn streaks from a laser Pistol about six inches on the left side of her torso.

He put some pressure on the wound, trying to stop the bleeding, but she had lost a lot of blood already. Ethan held her hand, saying, "Hey, I need you to put some pressure on the wound for me while I go get help, okay?"

Sarah didn't respond; she was losing consciousness. With trembling fingers, Ethan fumbled with Sarah's hologram communicator, his voice ragged as he pleaded for medical assistance from the Temporal Defense Org.

A rustle in the nearby forest sent a jolt of primal fear through Ethan. His heart hammered against his ribs. Suddenly, three soldiers, different from who he had seen before, emerged from the woods. He instinctively tried reaching for his HEL pistol, but before he could pull his pistol out, a blur of light slammed into him, knocking him to the ground. Ethan was left with a laser wound.

Dazed and wounded, Ethan scrambled to his knees and moved behind a nearby mound as the three Soldiers approached; finally grasping his HEL Pistol, he aimed and returned fire, hitting one and dropping him to the ground. The other two scrambled, and the battle ensued. Ethan, being pinned down by the two remaining soldiers, felt helpless as Sarah lay silent on the ground.

The Soldiers continued to advance, and then suddenly, the familiar uniforms of the Temporal Defense team materialized, their arrival ripping through the temporal distortion like a lifeline thrown across a sea, their blasters returning fire as they gave chase, sending the unfamiliar Soldiers escaping into the wood line.

Ethan sprinted towards Sarah while putting his HEL Pistol back in its case. Ignoring the throbbing ache in his shoulder, Ethan sank to his knees beside her. Her eyes fluttered.

"Sarah… Hey… Are you there?" She was faintly breathing. Pulling out the handkerchief from his pocket, he pressed against the crimson flow of blood from her wound to stop the bleeding.

Suddenly, one of the lead Agents knelt beside them, assessing the wound. "We need to get her back to headquarters now," he barked, his voice a reassuring anchor in the swirling chaos.

Time blurred into a montage of hurried movements, Sarah being gently lifted onto a stretcher, a cold compress pressed against her wound. With a final shudder, the portal snapped shut, leaving only the faint echoes of their desperate struggle behind. At the headquarters, the Medical team swarmed Sarah with their precise movements and practiced and treated her.

After being treated for her wounds, Sarah was now said to be in a stable state. Relieved that his shoulder wound, now neatly bandaged, wasn't serious, Ethan went to check up on her.

Weakened from her injuries, she placed a frail hand on his arm and said, "The group of soldiers we encountered, they're an extremely malicious group of people, even more dangerous than the Temporal Renegades that go by the name Temporal Conflux. They are responsible for all the Temporal anomalies in the timeline. Their enigmatic agenda is to rewrite history and wreak havoc."

Ethan was stunned to know that there were people besides the Temporal Renegades who wanted nothing but to disrupt the timeline. Standing beside Sarah's bedside, his heart was heavy with the weight of her words.

"Who are they?" Ethan asked, his voice tight and apprehensive.

"We don't know much yet," she admitted. "Our intel is fragmented, gathered from whispers and rumors on the fringes of the Virtual Dark Web. But we know that they are a ruthless group of people, determined to rewrite history to their liking and pose a significant threat to our lives."

"Ethan," she rasped, her voice thick with emotion, "there's no time to waste. Team Conflux is a viper in the timestream, and we must sever its head before it poisons the very fabric of existence." She continued, "I'm running on fumes at the moment; you're gonna have to go forward without me, rookie."

"I won't let you down, Sarah," he vowed, his voice firm despite the tremor in his heart. "I'll find Team Conflux and expose their truth, no matter the cost."

Sarah offered him a wan smile. "I know you will, Ethan," she said. "You have the courage of a lion and the heart of a true protector. Remember, the echoes of destiny will guide you further and lead you to your destination. Trust your instincts, and never lose sight of what's right."

As Ethan left Sarah's side, the weight of responsibility settled heavily upon his shoulders. He knew this journey would be perilous, but he was undeterred. He would unravel the secrets of Team Conflux, discover the truth about Zin Xia's erasure from history, and safeguard the timeline from those who sought to manipulate it for their nefarious ends.

His path would lead him through treacherous landscapes of time, from the glittering sprawl of neo-futuristic cities to the dust-choked ruins of forgotten civilizations. He would face cunning adversaries and navigate perilous temporal anomalies while grappling with the mysteries of Zen Xia's past. Most importantly, he was not alone. The echoes of destiny resonated within him, guiding him forward. He carried the hopes of his fallen comrade and the unwavering trust of his mentors. His journey had just begun, and the corridors of time awaited.

Ethan had to receive enhanced training at the Temporal Defense Org, pushing his body and mind to their limits. Ethan's days were a blur of holographic simulations, weapons drills, and strategic lectures. Every element of his training was meticulously designed to make him a weapon and to enable him to fortify himself against Temporal Conflux and stop them.

During his investigations into temporal anomalies caused by the Temporal Conflux, Ethan encountered a girl amidst the neon chaos of a bustling marketplace. She stood out like a luminous bloom in the shadows. Her hair, the color of spun moonlight, cascaded down her shoulders, framing eyes that shimmered with wisdom. An aura of effortless charm surrounded Lyra, a subtle magnetism that drew Ethan in like a moth to a flame.

"Looking for something, Temporal Agent?" she spoke, her voice a melody.

Ethan's hand instinctively reached for the HEL pistol strapped to his thigh. "I'm here to investigate the temporal anomalies," he said, his voice firm despite the unease. "They're causing chaos, eroding the fabric of time."

Lyra tilted her head, a mischievous sparkle in her eyes. "Chaos is a ladder, Agent. Sometimes, a little disruption is necessary for progress." Ethan frowned. "Progress at what cost? Innocent lives are at stake!"

Lyra's smile turned enigmatic. "Perhaps the cost of understanding the true nature of time itself. The Conflux is more than just a tear, Agent. It's a gateway to possibilities beyond your wildest dreams. My name is Lyra, by the way."

Ethan was intrigued; how did she know so much about it all? He replied, "I am Ethan". This wasn't the typical anomaly investigation. Lyra was no ordinary anomaly, and the Conflux, it seemed, held secrets far greater than he ever imagined.

He couldn't explain it but felt insatiable curiosity towards Lyra. Every word she spoke was like a riddle begging to be unraveled. He yearned to know the stories etched in her eyes, the mysteries hidden behind her smile. Despite their initial distrust, Ethan and Lyra formed an unlikely bond. Lyra's adherence to the harsh reality of survival of the fittest stood in stark contrast to Ethan's more idealistic upbringing within the Temporal Defense Org.

Hours passed away as they debated the nature of time, the disruption, and the potential hidden within the chaotic anomaly. "Lyra, your philosophies are captivating, but I can't shake the belief that humans are inherently evil in the world," Ethan said to Lyra.

"Ethan, you cling to the illusion of good and bad, a crutch for a world desperately seeking absolutes. But the truth, like time, is a river in constant flux. What's good today may be evil tomorrow, depending on the perspective you choose to wear," Lyra responded calmly.

"But surely there are fundamental principles, a moral compass that guides us. Can't we agree on some basic tenets of right and wrong?"

"Perhaps," Lyra conceded, a flicker of amusement in her eyes. "But who defines those tenets? The victors? The powerful? Morality is a fragile construct, easily shattered by the winds of time and circumstance."

Ethan pleaded, "But without it, what are we left with? Chaos? A world where might make right?"

"Not necessarily chaos," she countered, her voice softening. "Perhaps a beautiful, messy tapestry woven from the threads of countless perspectives. Maybe the absence of absolutes allows for greater understanding and empathy for the complexities that shape our choices."

"I... I suppose I never considered it that way; you challenge me, Lyra, in ways I never expected."

"And that, my dear Ethan, is the start of true wisdom."

Ethan felt the pull as he noticed Lyra lean forward. A war raged within him. Lyra's lips, soft and inviting, seemed to promise a thrilling escape from the weight of his duty, a glimpse into a reality where time flowed differently. Just as Ethan's lips were about to meet Lyra's, Zin Xia's message echoed in Ethan's ear, and he quickly leaned back. A surge of guilt flooded his system, the taste of ashes in his mouth. He had a mission, a promise, and indulging in this seductive distraction would be an unforgivable dereliction of duty and his commitments.

A smirk played on Lyra's lips, unfazed by Ethan's outrage, almost as if she expected it coming. "See, Ethan? Your precious morals bind you, mere shackles on your true potential. Freedom lies beyond them, in the raw power you refuse to embrace."

Ethan was now infuriated; he couldn't take it anymore. He surged to his feet, his anger a palpable force. As he whirled around, ready to confront Lyra's callous statement, a ripple of distortion passed through the place when a group of people appeared straight out of thin air. They surrounded Ethan from every corner. Dressed in stark white uniforms, their faces hidden behind emotionless masks.

"Who are you people?" Ethan roared, his voice echoing in the sudden silence. His heart pounded against his ribs as the figures in white stared down at him, their presence suffocating. A familiar giggle came out from nearby, and Lyra emerged from between these people.

"Lyra? You... you're with them?" His voice cracked, the tremor betraying his disbelief. "We are the Temporal Conflux, and I am the head operative," she replied with a smirk on her face. The weight of her betrayal was crushing him; he was left dumbfounded. As he struggled to pick his words, he grunted.

He didn't know what was about to happen next, and then he just reached out to his pocket, pressing the emergency device's button to call for assistance from Temporal Defense. He tried to pull out his HEL Pistol when his hands were seized by two of the members of Temporal Conflux.

"What do you guys want?" he yelled. "We want just one simple thing, Ethan, that is to reshape the tapestry of time itself, rewrite its narrative to fit our vision.", Lyra replied.

"But why? Who could justify erasing lives, manipulating the past for their own gain?"

Her smile fading, replaced by a steely glint, Lyra said, "Justification, Ethan, is a luxury reserved for the weak. We see the future fragmented and perilous. And to safeguard our own existence, we must prune the branches that threaten to trap us. Those who stand in our way are... eliminated."

With his fists clenched, anger sparking in his eyes, "Eliminated? You talk about people like they're insects to be squashed! You have no right to play God with the lives of others!"

"Right and wrong, my dear, are mere constructs of time itself. And when you seize the reins of time, such concepts become... malleable. Perhaps your perspective will change once you understand the true threat we face."

Like a puzzle finally resolving into a horrifying image, Ethan finally had the realization. He could now grasp the chilling truth behind Zin Xia's disappearance from the timestream and all the other Temporal anomalies.

Ethan was forced to kneel down with his hands now tied to his back by these figures. "Ethan, your heroic intentions pose a significant threat to us, and you must be terminated," Lyra said monotonously. He was now terrified. Lyra casually grabbed a HEL Pistol, holding its barrel, aimed directly at his forehead, pulsated with an ominous inner light.

Time seemed to slow down, each beat of his terrified heart a hammer blow against his ribs. His memories flashed before his eyes: Zin Xia's determined smile and his promise to her, Sarah's belief and expectation in him, his time at Temporal Defense Org, the thrill of the chase, the weight of responsibility. He closed his eyes, and suddenly, he heard a HEL Pistol getting fired…

Chapter 12: Threads Intertwined

For a moment, there was a silence followed by the sound of HEL Pistol noise. With his eyes closed, Ethan could only hear his ears ringing. Unaware of what had happened, he opened his eyes to see the familiar uniform of the Temporal Defense team combatting against Temporal Conflux. Ethan squinted, his vision swimming in the relentless glare of the HEL Pistols. The darkness covered the edges of his sight, like a vignette frame, obscuring the view.

In an effort to locate Lyra, he rubbed his eyes, but she was nowhere to be found. He instantly knew that she had escaped already. Ethan swiftly yanked his HEL Pistol from the ground nearby, his frustration now replaced by grim determination. He joined the Temporal Defense team to fight the Temporal Conflux. The fight persisted for a few minutes when one of the Temporal Conflux Soldiers opened a portal, and in what seemed like a dizzying flash of light, the whole team vanished into thin air.

One of the soldiers from Temporal Defense approached Ethan. "Are you hurt?" he assessed his body, searching for any wounds or injuries.

"No, I'm okay.", he replied with a sigh. "But she has escaped!"

"Who are you talking about?" the soldier asked.

"Her name is Lyra. She is the head operative of Team Conflux," he responded with a grunt. "She tricked me!"

Then, Ethan, using his Chronos Resurgence device, opened a portal back to the Temporal Conflux headquarters, and they all left.

Ethan's initial anger curdled into a bitter cocktail of guilt and loss. It started to consume him from inside, each accusing glare from a teammate adding another brick to the wall of self-blame. His mind replayed the events on a loop, each misstep amplified by his shame. How could he let this happen? How could he be so careless? He felt that he had let Zin Xia, Sarah, and the whole team down.

In the headquarters, Sarah awaited him. Her wounds had healed, and she was in a much better condition. Despite the weight of guilt, there was a glimmer of hope because Sarah was there. Maybe he could find forgiveness, or at least a way to be saved, in her eyes. Her steadfast devotion might be what he needs to weather the internal storm.

"Hey, rookie! Long day, huh?" she asked Ethan with a cheerful tone in her voice. Ethan was relieved now. He could tell that she was not upset or felt like he had let the team down.

"Yeah, definitely a long and exhausting day". He replied with a slight grin, raising one corner of his lips.

"I can imagine," she responded, "You should get some rest. You're going to need it. The team will be having a meeting in the morning, so you have to be up early."

"Okay. I'm gonna get some sleep.", Ethan said, stretching his arms.

Lying on the single bed of his assigned shared bedroom with three other members of the Temporal Defense, Ethan stared at the ceiling. Distracted by inadvertently hearing his teammates conversing in the room, he tried closing his eyes to think.

As the guilt and fear of letting the team down slowly receded like the tides on a stormy coast, he could finally think clearly. He started pondering about what Lyra told him. Her words echoed inside his head. What if what she said is true? What if the good or bad are mere illusions, but it's just a matter of perspectives? What if he had the power to manipulate reality himself? If he could rewrite history, would he still choose to be good? But what does being good really mean? A battle started inside his head, and he did not feel like sleeping anymore.

Lyra had definitely stirred his beliefs, but the concerning thing was he could not stop thinking about her. He couldn't deny the spark he felt around her, the way her fiery passion ignited something within him. Was it a matter of curiosity or something more profound? He felt a growing fear of losing his identity and mission to someone who might be his enemy as a result of the uncertainty that was eating away at him.

The night stretched on like an eternity, each tick of the clock echoing Ethan's internal turmoil. Doubts gnawed at him, and Lyra's words continued echoing in his mind like a haunting melody. When sleep did eventually arrive, it brought with it jumbled dreams with hazy faces. He was tired when he woke up, and his sleepless night was evident in the dark circles under his eyes.

The next morning, every member of the team reported to the conference room for the meeting. There, Ethan opened up about his experience with encountering Lyra and Team Conflux. As he spoke, Ethan felt a constant battle raging within. The urge to confess his internal turmoil, the nagging doubts fueled by Lyra, warred with the fear of revealing weaknesses and jeopardizing his trust. He maintained a composed facade, yet a flicker of apprehension in his eyes hinted at the unspoken truth.

"We have enough intel on Temporal Conflux now to start preparing our defenses. We still have to find out their vulnerability and work on our strategy to fight against them", the head executive's words painted a stark picture of the impending conflict. "The meeting is dismissed!"

Ethan was now assigned on a mission to go back in history to unravel the tangled origin of Team Conflux and look for their weak spots. He was now accompanied by Sarah on this mission, and it felt nice to have his comrade back with him. He had managed to repress his thoughts from that night and was now more focused than ever.

A montage of his memories with Zin Xia kept replaying in his head. He missed her immensely, but remembering her message, he knew their paths would intertwine soon. The thought of Zin Xia fueled Ethan's determination again for the mission. He knew that the roads would soon lead him back to her.

Arriving at the moment in history when it was believed that the head guy of Temporal Conflux discovered a Chronos Resurgence, which later led to havoc in the timeline. They were in the ruins of a place that used to be a huge city. The city sprawled like a skeletal giant, its bones bleached white by the desert sun. Dust accumulated in the empty sockets, and whispering winds hummed through its hollow ribs.

A faint crunching echoed amidst the ruins, drawing Ethan's attention. Delicate rock fragments crumbled beneath unseen footsteps, the sound sharp and distinct in the oppressive silence. "Sarah, I hear footsteps around here," he whispered to her.

They both pulled out their HEL Pistols, now slowly maneuvering across the stack of broken pillars while trying to stay inconspicuous. "It's coming from inside that place," Sarah said, pointing towards what seemed like a skeletal remains husk of an old house, now resembling a cave. Both maneuvered their way to the entrance and took a peek inside that place.

It was a boy, barely eight years old, in a torn-up white shirt, now yellowed by the dirt and the dust. He was holding an artifact, and Ethan knew it was a Chronos Resurgence. "Hurry! We have to stop him before he opens the portal," he whispered to Sarah.

"No, Ethan. We're not here to stop him. We're just here to observe." Sarah responded.

"But Sarah, this is the moment. The genesis of the evil itself is in front of us. We can't just watch and let it happen." Ethan exclaimed.

"We don't want to change the history and have unwanted turbulence in the timeline. You know it's our one and only rule at Temporal Defense," she replied with a weight in her voice.

"So we're just gonna let him get away?" Ethan asked in anger.

"We have to!"

At that very moment, a flash of light erupted from the house's depths, momentarily swallowing the boy in its white fury. As the brilliance receded, the boy was gone, vanishing like smoke on the wind, leaving only a lingering echo of his presence.

Ethan was now infuriated. It just didn't make any sense to him. Why let him get away even though they knew that he would lead to the origin of Team Conflux and would be responsible for all the chaos and catastrophe later? He wondered what the worst that could happen if they disrupted the timeline. He just had this uncontrollable urge to want to be in control and to have power.

After returning back to the headquarters, Ethan's faith had been shaken. It was like Pandora's box had opened, and he started to wonder what it would be like to have power. Lyra's words echoed in his head: "Right and wrong are mere constructs of time itself. And when you seize the reins of time, such concepts become... malleable."

Her words did make sense. It was all a matter of perspective. He had questions, lots of them, that he wanted to ask Lyra. Interestingly, he had this insatiable urge to meet Lyra again and confront her about this.

After informing the team about what they saw, Ethan returned to his assigned bedroom to rest for the night. While staring at the ceiling, the thought crossed his mind: what if he could travel back in time to the moment he met Lyra? But he knew that Team Conflux wanted him killed. The weird, unsteady feeling started to tickle him internally, and soon, he yielded to the urge. Getting up from his bed, he found his way to the door in the dimly lit room.

It was the middle of the night, and everyone at the headquarters was fast asleep. In an almost trance-like state, he made his way to the control room, which usually was heavily guarded during the day. Surprisingly, it was empty at night. As he got inside the room, his eyes scanned the control desk, frantic in his search for the Chronos Resurgence, which now was allowed only to those authorized to use it under team supervision or for the assigned missions. There it was, in the center of the main control desk, its peculiar ancient shape standing out against the futuristic control panel.

Ethan seized the Chronos Resurgence; it pulsated with power in his hands, and its cold surface was almost satisfying to touch. Uncertain and indecisive about his plan, he had internal turmoil about whether he should do this or not. He knew he was going against the laws of Temporal Defense and betraying his own team. What would Sarah think? Would Zin Xia still accept him knowing this fact?

But his relentless curiosity was much stronger than the sense of guilt or fear he was feeling. Before he knew it, his hands had already activated the Chronos Resurgence, almost as if they had a mind of their own. In a vortex of blinding light and a sense of vertigo, he had traveled back to the point where he met Lyra.

There she was, standing in the neon light, with an almost apparition-like presence, with her hair slightly moving in the wind's direction. Before he could approach her, Ethan froze; his eyes widened, and his throat narrowed as he witnessed his past self there already. Their initial conversation had already started, playing almost like a recording in front of his eyes.

He had the irresistible urge to jump in between them and have Lyra surrender. But he didn't want to mess with the timeline. What he could do was wait until his past self was seized by the Temporal Conflux, and once the Temporal Defense team was there, he would follow Lyra into her portal as she escaped.

Time passed, and Ethan was still there in the distance, completely inconspicuous, hiding behind a tower. He was tired and was slowly starting to drift away; his eyelids were drooping heavily, and the world around him began to blur and fade. Just as fatigue was about to pull him into the depths of slumber, a sharp crack in the distance jolted him. It was the sound of a HEL Pistol.

He instantly knew it was when the Temporal Defense team arrived. He had to locate Lyra, and there she was, hiding behind a storage container, trying to activate her Chronos Resurgence. No conscious thought fueled his actions. Ethan all but sprinted towards Lyra in a blur of desperate motion, and just as the flash of light was about to engulf her, he plunged into it. When the light subsided, both he and Lyra had vanished into thin air...

Chapter 13: Weaver's Web

After a dizzying spell, Ethan opened his eyes, only to reveal a blurry vision of the surroundings. His head was pounding like a drum, almost as if his brain was about to escape his skull. These kinds of feelings and sensations were common after a huge leap in the timeline while time traveling. After repeatedly rubbing his eyes in an effort to make sense of the surroundings, his vision finally cleared up a little.

There he was in a somewhat futuristic cityscape of breathtaking fusion of gleaming technology and ancient wonders. Towering spires reach towards the sky, their surfaces shimmering with a soft, iridescent glow reminiscent of moonlight. Each building was a masterpiece of architectural innovation, seamlessly blending modern materials with the timeless elegance of ancient stonework.

The whole view was surreal and breathtaking, but there was a haze, darkness, and almost some kind of malevolence in the city. On the top of a skyscraper, there was a holographic LED screen with a running bulletin that echoed through the atmosphere: "Welcome to the Lumina Era, where the past meets the future. Please enjoy your time here."

Recalling how he came here, Ethan looked around to locate Lyra in the surrounding cityscape, but she was long gone. She was elusive, like time itself. Ethan was exasperated. Deciding whether he should travel back to the headquarters or look for Lyra here, he felt the cityscape calling out his name, waiting to be explored. There was some kind of magnetic pull that lured him into the city.

"Please enjoy your time here!" the bulletin echoed again.

Ethan's senses were drawn in by more than just the cityscape. Hidden sanctuaries with ancient temples standing in silent homage to a bygone era can be found beyond the busy streets. There is a sense of wonder and reverence in their hallowed halls as soft machinery hums along with the essence of the past.

As he explored this vivid world, Ethan was drawn to the Lumina District, which was the center of the city. The streets here are lined with tall pillars that have been ornately carved to tell a tale from a bygone era. Market stalls beneath the enormous holographic displays, which showcase the newest technological innovations, are bursting at the seams with treasures from both old and new.

"Are you lost, Temporal Agent?" a familiar voice came in from behind him, instinctively making the hair on his neck stand.

Recognizing the voice, Ethan quickly turned his head, and there she was, with her nonchalant demeanor, looking at him with slightly tilted lips and that signature grin.

"Lyra!" Ethan, panicking, called out while trying to grab his HEL Pistol.

"Don't bother Ethan! We've been here before, haven't we?" Lyra said in her husky yet slightly melodious voice.

Ethan fumbled. He was filled with emotions that were a mix of fear and anger.

"I knew you were gonna come back. I'm sure you have a lot of questions. But I want to show you something first." Lyra told him with a sense of superiority in her voice.

"What makes you think I would listen to you?" Ethan grunted.

"Well, you're here to meet me, aren't you?" she responded.

He was stunned to find out that Lyra already knew he was going to come back. But he had to know the truth. This was, after all, what he came here for.

"How do I know I can even trust you?" he asked Lyra with a grunt, an endeavor to mask his uncertainty.

"You will once we get there," Lyra replied.

Following Lyra's lead, he started walking behind her with his one hand clasped against the HEL Pistol's case on his right leg. After crossing a series of tall ancient monuments and buildings, they stopped by a skyscraper, gray with no visible windows, towering over the sky like some kind of entity.

"Welcome to the Temporal Conflux's headquarters!" said Lyra in a rather cheerful tone, which was unusual for her normally conniving demeanor.

"Wait! Why are you taking me here?" Ethan asked in utter suspicion.

"You wanted the truth about the Temporal Conflux, right?" Lyra asked. "Here it is."

Ethan felt a knot of anxiety tighten in his stomach. Though he had no idea what Lyra was playing at, standing still felt just as dangerous. The place was heavily guarded, with soldiers with their signature stark white uniforms and emotionless helmets covering their faces. He was met with an unsettling quiet, only to be disturbed by the steady thump of his own heart. Nobody moved or asked him a question. It almost seemed like, in a way, he was expected to be there.

Lyra led him through the cold and silent corridors of the headquarters into a door that led to a large conference room. Ethan's heart was thumping out of his chest, fear gnawing at him that any moment he could be attacked or, worse, be held captive by the Temporal Conflux soldiers.

"Don't worry! No one will hurt you", Lyra told him, almost as if she could read through his thoughts like an open book. "You're safe here, Ethan." Her voice held a weight of comfort in it, which eventually made Ethan lower his guard.

Lyra started to unravel the Temporal Conflux's convoluted past and told him the story of its mysterious creator, the Temporal Weaver. Not only was he a leader, but he was also the mastermind behind their whole setup, with his influence permeating the organization's core. He had the power to manipulate time and was responsible for all the Temporal anomalies caused by the Temporal Conflux.

Ethan's brain clicked; he was the same guy he and Sarah had encountered in the ruins. He was the one who started it all: the chaos, the mayhem, and the destruction. He found himself drawn deeper into the labyrinthine machinations of the Temporal Conflux, realizing that the key to unraveling their secrets might lie within the grasp of this enigmatic figure: the Temporal Weaver.

She leaned in closer, her voice dwindling to a whisper of conspiracy. "Darling, it's all about the power," she said, her eyes beaming with desire. "Power over time itself. Consider the universe as your sandbox, customized to suit your every desire."

"But that doesn't make any sense!" Ethan groaned.

She chuckled with a hint of darkness in her laughter. "Forget causes, forget heroes. A child is the truest master, unburdened by rules or consequences. That's the notion of Temporal Weaver and the kind of freedom we strive for.' Her gaze flickered, momentarily revealing a vulnerability beneath the facade. Fascination possessed Ethan's mind.

"Imagine," she whispered, her hand touching his like a feather on the skin, "What if the reins of time were offered to you? No strings attached, no consequences to fear. History, the future, a blank canvas at your fingertips. Would you dare to paint your masterpiece?"

"What are you proposing, Lyra?" Ethan asked with his eyes wide open, almost as if he had been hypnotized by Lyra's words.

"We're offering you the chance to join Temporal Conflux and become the force that shapes the universe. Don't just be a narrative; be the writer himself, and write the timeline to fit your wildest fantasies," she responded.

He was dumbfounded. Was this really happening? Joining Temporal Conflux, possessing unimaginable power? But he recalled his commitments and responsibility to Temporal defense. How could he betray them with such ease, given the trust she held in him? Though temptation roared, he was restrained by the bonds of responsibility.

He tried thinking about his promise to Zin Xia, their memories together, but now it all felt like a distant memory, clouded by everything that had happened in his life recently. Stuck in a battle raging inside his head, he felt the weight of anxiety crushing him; it was paralyzing.

Ethan stood stock still, his mind reeling. Joining Temporal Conflux felt like a betrayal, yet curiosity was getting the best of him. No doubt, he was fueled by Lyra's captivating offer. Her hand, cool and smooth, brushed against his. "Come," she murmured, her voice hypnotic. "Let me show you the truth."

Ethan hesitated, but the yearning for knowledge and the desire to understand proved stronger. He nodded, sealing his pact with fate. Lyra smiled, a glint of triumph in her eyes. Grasping a shimmering orb etched with intricate symbols, she activated the Chronos Resurgence. A swirl of energy engulfed them, ripping them from the present and propelling them through the vortex of time.

The world morphed around them. Ancient pyramids materialized, their golden surfaces gleaming under a sun long extinguished. Ethan glimpsed pharaohs and priests performing cryptic rituals, anomalies shimmering in the air like heat mirages. Lyra narrated, her voice echoing through the ages, pointing out temporal ripples of history.

They hurtled through epochs, witnessing the rise and fall of empires, the birth of groundbreaking inventions, and pivotal moments marred by temporal distortions. Medieval knights clashed with shimmering energy shields, and futuristic skyscrapers crumbled under the weight of anachronistic storms.

Ethan felt dwarfed by the immense scale of time, his mind struggling to comprehend the implications of these anomalies. Each glimpse chipped away at his understanding of reality, leaving him both awed and unsettled.

Finally, they arrived in a future shrouded in an ominous, metallic sheen. Towering megacities scraped the sky, pulsating with artificial light. Yet, shadows lurked amidst the neon glow, a sense of unease permeating the very air. Here, too, anomalies danced like malevolent specters, hinting at a future teetering on the brink.

Lyra's hand tightened on his, her voice grave. "All these anomalies are the creation of Temporal Weaver, our leader," she said.

Exhausted and overwhelmed, Ethan stared at the desolate landscape. The offer echoed in his ears. What if he decides to join Temporal Conflux? Soon, they were back at the Temporal Conflux headquarters.

Leading him through the corridor, Lyra took Ethan inside what seemed to be some sort of control room. "He is ready to meet you now?" Lyra told him.

"Who is?" Ethan questioned.

A voice boomed from the near distance: "Welcome, Ethan! We've been waiting for you."

Startled, Ethan restlessly started looking around to see where the voice was coming from. It was from the chair at the front, facing the large holographic screen on the wall. The chair spanned around, revealing a guy with a mature face, greyed hair on the sides, and a smile that seemed friendly yet startling.

Ethan wasn't sure what to say, and before he could utter a word, the guy continued, "I am Temporal Weaver, the head of Temporal Conflux."

He moved with a deliberate precision that befits his mastery of the temporal arts; even his suit appeared to be rippling with the currents of time itself. There he was, the kid Ethan and Sarah had encountered at the ruins, the man whose influence reverberated through the annals of history, rewriting the fabric of reality with every passing moment and shaping destinies...

Chapter 14: Desperate Gambit

For a moment, Ethan stood there silently, holding his breath. His skin appeared washed out by the harsh, luminescent white lights inside the control room. The creases between his brows deepened, and his frown became exaggerated. He felt the knot in his gut tightened. He was filled with mixed emotions as standing right before him was the Temporal Weaver, the architect of all the chaos and destruction that the entire Temporal Defense team had been fighting against the whole time.

"How do you know my name?" Ethan groaned.

"I know a lot more about you than your name, Ethan. Come take a seat!" the Temporal Weaver responded with a friendly grin.

Ethan, initially hesitant, decided to sit down and listen to what he had to say.

"You know Ethan, initially I was hesitant about you, but you have managed to really surprise me. Little did I know that sending Lyra to find you would turn out to be a fruitful decision."

"What do you mean by that?" Ethan paused for a moment, pondering about it. "So it was all part of the elaborate plan from the first time Lyra first met me?"

"Yes. But try looking at the bright side, Ethan, how it finally brought you here to Temporal Conflux, to me, exactly where you belong."

"I do not belong here!" Ethan yelled defiantly.

"Don't lie to yourself, Ethan. You are better than that. You were tempted to know more about us. You came here on your own 'cause you wanted this."

Ethan was speechless; he didn't know how to respond. He sat there like a deer in the headlight, quietly biting the inside of his cheek until he felt a metallic taste in his mouth. Realizing that he had cut the skin, he felt it with his tongue, feeling the slight burn, but he was too distracted by the pounding heart in his chest.

"You possess immense potential in you, Ethan; you just need to channel and harness it. Think of what you could build across the timelines, unhindered by limits or consequence," said the Temporal Weaver with his voice laced with promises.

A storm was building inside of Ethan. The sweet and promising words of the Temporal Weaver presented a world of unbridled creativity and wild power. Unquestionably, the idea was enticing, luring him in the direction of the limitless potential that was simmering inside of him. However, there was a counterpoint, a quiet whisper, in the back of his mind. It was Zin Xia's voice, imprinted in his mind, a reminder of their relationship and cherished promise. Then, another face appeared in his thoughts of Sarah, his companion. How could he break her trust in him?

With a steely glint in his eyes, Ethan leaped out of the chair with determination. "I'm getting out of here. I won't be swayed by your empty promises!" he said, his voice piercing through the devoid atmosphere of the control room. "The Temporal Defense will hunt you down, and you'll face the consequences of your actions!"

The Temporal Weaver erupted in laughter, a harsh, mocking cackle that echoed through the control room like a broken record on fast-forward. "Oh, you will be staying," he rasped, his voice dripping with false sincerity, "we can't simply let you walk out of here now, not after you've discovered my identity. Seize him!"

A squad of Temporal Conflux soldiers materialized in a flash of motion, their stark white uniforms gleaming in the control room's harsh light. They moved with chilling precision, encircling Ethan like wolves closing in on prey. With a swiftness born of brutal efficiency, they disarmed him, seizing his HEL pistol and the Chronos Resurgence from his possession. They put cuffs around his wrists and dragged him toward a cell, which looked like a hologram cube with see-through walls.

A primal urge to fight rushed through Ethan. His muscles screamed in protest as he strained against the restraints. With the hope of escape clouding his mind, he lunged toward the shimmering wall. But a sharp shock surged through his entire body when his fingertips touched the holographic barrier. The impact was so intense that it caused him to lose consciousness and spiral into a state of dizziness. His resistance broke, and he collapsed to the ground, unconscious.

After a couple of hours, Ethan gained consciousness and was greeted by Lyra, who was standing outside his cell looking at him remorselessly. He got up on his feet and went closer to the wall she was standing by.

"Careful! You don't want to get yourself shocked by the current again!" Lyra said with her signature smirk.

"You are a terrible person, Lyra. You're not gonna get away with this!" Ethan yelled.

"You know Ethan, it's such a loss, a tragedy. I really believed for a moment that you would be a smart guy and make the right decision."

"If by the right decision, you mean to join the Temporal Conflux, I would never." He continued: "Yes! I faltered for a moment, but you manipulated me, twisting my vulnerabilities. Now that the dust has finally settled, I see it all crystal clear, and I see you guys for what you really are!"

A cruel smirk twisted Lyra's features, followed by a harsh, humorless laugh. "But it's too late now, dear."

Desperate and helpless, Ethan groaned, and a guttural growl escaped his throat. He had the irresistible urge to jump at her, but the shimmering current in the holographic walls stopped him, and he just stood there paralyzed.

The concept of time fractured in the cell. Days bled into nights, or so Ethan assumed. The relentless white light offered no clue to the rhythm of the world beyond the prison walls. He felt like a specimen pinned under a harsh microscope, dissected by his own despair.

Hope, once a fierce ember in his chest, began to dwindle. The thought of Sarah storming in to save him with the Temporal Defense faded like a fleeting dream. He grappled with escape plans, each one collapsing under the crushing weight of reality that he was alone, a lone warrior against the vast, oppressive power of the Temporal Conflux. The burden of his isolation slowly started to consume him.

A few weeks passed, and just when he was finally starting to yield to his fate, he heard a sound that broke the oppressive monotony. There was a distinct, sharp crack that could only be made by a HEL pistol. Before long, there was another shot that reverberated throughout the clean room. He shot to his feet, driven onward by a fresh sense of purpose. The holographic cell wall that had previously been impenetrable shimmered and vanished, exposing an open doorway.

Just when he was about to escape, he saw a figure approaching him in the blinding lights. His eyes widened in disbelief. It couldn't be. Standing before him, defiant and resolute, was Zin Xia.

"Hello, Ethan! I told you we would meet again." Said Zin Xia. Her voice almost resuscitated Ethan from his despair.

"Zin Xia, you're really here." He responded with a shaking voice, trying to hold back the tears that were forming behind his eyes. "But how did you find me?"

"I received a message from the Temporal Defense telling me about your unexpected disappearance from the headquarters. They have been looking for you for a while. When they told me about your encounter with the Temporal Conflux, I knew you'd be in trouble, and it was about time until I found their headquarters."

"Yeah, Zin Xia, I made a big mistake!" he responded with his voice filled with sorrow.

"We have to hurry up now, Ethan, before they notice anything. The Temporal Defense team is on their way to rescue you."

Zin Xia pulled out a HEL Pistol from her case and handed it to Ethan as they both tried sneaking through the corridor. Suddenly, a familiar voice came from behind them: "Leaving too soon, Ethan?"

As Ethan spun around, his heart lurched. Before him stood the Temporal Weaver, flanked by a smirking Lyra and a horde of Temporal Conflux soldiers ready for the kill. Before he could raise his HEL pistol, a searing pain erupted in his leg. A soldier had fired, taking him down, but luckily, the laser didn't pierce his flesh. Instead, it ricocheted off his leg, leaving a scorch mark. With a groan that fell out of his mouth, he fell to one knee.

Just as the Temporal Conflux was about to close in, the air warped and distorted as a bright light filled the room. As the light subsided, familiar figures materialized. It was the Temporal Defense team, and at their forefront stood Sarah, her eyes filled with fierce determination. The tide had turned, and the battle for Ethan's freedom had just begun.

Sarah rushed towards him with lightning speed, conjuring a holographic shield around to protect him. Zin Xia, along with the rest of the soldiers of Temporal Defense, started to battle Temporal Conflux, and the sound of HEL Pistols echoed throughout the room. The clash was a symphony of temporal forces, each movement a desperate gambit to reshape the very fabric of existence.

"I have to get Temporal Weaver. He is the one in control of the Temporal Conflux's entire operation!" Ethan told Sarah as she put a bandage on his wounded leg.

Rising to his feet, Ethan winced from the burning ache in his leg. Across the battle scene, his eyes met Temporal Weaver's, a flicker of defiance momentarily challenging him. Seizing his HEL Pistol, he shot at Weaver, but he dodged the fire almost as if he knew where it was going to hit. He looked back at him with a condescending grin. Ethan was furious.

"Here, Ethan, grab this HEL Pistol too!" Sarah said while throwing another pistol at him.

With a surge of adrenaline, Ethan grasped both HEL Pistols and lunged toward the Temporal Weaver. However, the Temporal Weaver seemed to possess an uncanny precognition, almost as if he could slow down the time, and before the beams of energy could even come close, he effortlessly dodged and weaved through the attack. Weaver didn't even have a weapon on him. It was almost as if he was immune to the HEL Pistol beam. Before Ethan could fire at him again, Lyra showed up in the middle and fired at Ethan. It was too close for comfort, but he managed to dodge the beam by just a few milliseconds and fell to his knees.

During this final desperate gambit, Zin Xia and Sarah channeled the power of the Chronos Resurgence. The air crackled with temporal energy, and reality seemed to tremble as the forces of preservation clashed with the forces of manipulation. For a moment, time itself held its breath and slowed down.

With time seemingly bending around them, Ethan got up on his feet and charged towards the Temporal Weaver. The rest of the Temporal Conflux moved like figures caught in molasses, but the Weaver stood unaffected, almost as if the temporal energy didn't affect it. Ethan stood Face to face with Weaver, his locked eyes with his adversary.

"Ethan, you think you could finish me?" he said in a soft tone. "But I am immortal, and nothing can stop me!"

"I'm not gonna let you get away!' Ethan yelled.

Aiming his HEL Pistol at him, Ethan pulled the trigger. With a burst of bright light, Temporal Weaver vanished into thin air, and the beam fired through the empty space. Disbelief washed over him as he saw the space where the Temporal Weaver stood moments ago, and in that moment, the temporal force from the Chronos Resurgence got back to normal, and the battle continued to rage with laser fire and frantic cries.

Anger, raw and scorching, surged through Ethan. He whirled across the battle scene; Lyra's eyes met his as she fired at him. Dodging it, Ethan raised the weapon, aiming with calculated precision towards Lyra. The laser fired, a searing beam splitting the air. It found its mark, passing through Lyra's chest and leaving a gaping hole. Ethan's gaze met Lyra's one last time, and after a moment of disbelief and shock, she lost her balance and fell to the floor.

The Temporal Defense team battled with unwavering determination, gradually shifting the tide against the Temporal Conflux with their coordinated movements and refined skill. The soldiers in white uniforms fell one by one, their defiance fading. Before long, the group was reduced to a small number, with their backs to the wall. An act of desperation destroyed the momentum just as the Temporal Defense was closing in for the last assault. The few surviving soldiers of Temporal Conflux retreated and fled from the battle.

Ethan felt a wave of relief so strong that it almost knocked him off his feet. The battle was finally over, the sound of fatigue dying away and the stench of burnt metal lingering. The Temporal Defense team let out a collective sigh, lowering their weapons and starting to tend to the injured. Their faces were still serious.

Ethan saw Zin Xia walking toward him through the dust, her steps deliberate but measured. "Are you okay, Ethan?" she asked in the most comforting tone.

"Yes, Zin Xia. I'm okay, are you okay?"

"Yes, I am."

"I can't begin to tell you how grateful I am to you for rescuing me, Zin Xia. I had almost lost all my hope, thinking I would be trapped here forever. But you showed up like a miracle amidst the darkness." He said with his voice filled with gratitude and admiration. His gaze softened as they locked their eyes.

Sarah walked in during the middle of the conversation and told Ethan: "Come on. It's time to get you back home, Ethan."

"Hold on! Before they locked me up, they confiscated my Chronos Resurgence. We need to search the facility and find it before it falls into the wrong hands." Ethan responded in a concerned tone.

Chapter 15: The Nexus Point

Alarmed by Ethan's revelation that the Chronos Resurgence was missing, a collective sense of urgency gripped the Temporal Defense team. The entire team started rummaging through the Temporal Conflux headquarters, looking for the device, their movements sharp and purposeful. They swarmed every corner, their eyes scanning diligently for any sign of the elusive device. The hum of activity intensified as whispers and the clatter of equipment filled the air.

"Do you know where Temporal Weaver could have kept it?" asked Sarah.

"They seized it before they cuffed my hands in the control room," Ethan replied.

"But we have searched through every corner of the control room looking for it; we have found your HEL Pistol, but the Chronos Resurgence is not there," said one of the Temporal Defense Agents.

Panicking, Ethan thought about the possibility that Temporal Weaver might have fled with his Chronos Resurgence. The weight of this realization pressed down on Ethan. How could he confess his suspicions to the team? He envisioned their disappointment, their distrust. The thought of being ostracized, perhaps even permanently removed from Temporal Defense, a place he considered his home, was excruciating.

Amidst the frantic pandemonium, a flicker of hope sparked within Ethan. Could it be that the Chronos Resurgence wasn't lost after all? His gaze darted towards the lifeless form of Lyra sprawled on the cold floor, her signature grin now distorted into an eternal frown. He rushed towards her. With a heavy heart, he reached into her pockets, his fingers brushing against her frigid body, and then, a wave of relief washed over him. In her pocket lay the familiar, metallic outline of the Chronos Resurgence.

After seizing his Chronos Resurgence, the Temporal Defense team, Ethan and Zin Xia, finally returned to headquarters.

Returning to the familiar space of Temporal Defense headquarters felt like a balm to Ethan. Days of confinement in Temporal Weaver's cell, a concrete tomb devoid of natural light, had left him yearning for the familiar hum of activity and the comforting routine of his temporal defense duties. The entire team was given the time to get some rest after this event.

In the morning, Ethan opened his eyes in his appointed room to find Zin Xia sitting at the foot of his bed, looking at him.

"Hey, good morning!" said Zin Xia.

"Good morning, Zin Xia," Ethan replied with a faint smile.

"How did you sleep?" she asked.

"Like a baby," Ethan responded while rubbing his eyes. "You know, Zin Xia, when I was trapped in that cell, I had almost given up on the hope that I would get to see you again," he paused and continued, "But then, there you were, at the time I least expected, to rescue me from the mess that I walked into myself."

"Ethan, I had this premonition that something bad had happened to you. I just felt it in my heart," said Zin Xia while reaching out for Ethan's hand and grabbing it. "It wasn't until

Sarah found a way to reach out to me and told me that you had disappeared that I knew I had to find you."

"I am really grateful for you, Zin Xia," said Ethan, leaning forward toward Zin Xia until the space between them diminished, and their lips met in a kiss, a soft touch that spoke volumes of unspoken emotions.

Moments later, there was a knock on the door. It was a Temporary defense agent. "Ethan, you have been summoned for a meeting with the head," he told him.

Ethan felt anxiousness clawing him from the inside. It was finally time for the confrontation after everything that had happened. Taking a deep breath, he braced himself for the conversation. The head of Temporal Defense greeted him in the conference room.

"Son, do you realize what you have done and how detrimental it could have been for the entire Temporal Defense team?" he asked Ethan.

"Yes, sir. I made a big mistake, and I am really sorry about it," Ethan answered as he felt remorse for his actions.

"While your actions with the Chronos Resurgence placed Temporal Defense at significant risk, they also inadvertently revealed the truth about Temporal Weaver and offered valuable insights into the workings of Temporal Conflux. Recognizing this, the team has decided to issue you a formal warning. However, this incident serves as a stark reminder that similar lapses in judgment will not be tolerated in the future."

"Absolutely, sir. I fully understand the severity of the situation and the potential consequences my actions could have caused. I deeply regret what I have done and assure you that I will take every step necessary to ensure such an incident never occurs again."

"Good. Now, Ethan, we have a really crucial mission for you; we need you to get to the Nexus Point."

"The Nexus Point?"

"Yes, the Nexus Point is the place where past, present, and future intersect. That place plays a vital role in keeping harmony in the timeline, but at the moment, we have been told about a major threat posed by the Temporal Renegades and their audacious scheme. We have to stop them before they can tamper with the timeline."

"Yes, sir, I will ensure that we neutralize the threat and stop Temporal Renegades before anything happens to the Nexus Point."

A tense energy crackled through the Temporal Defense headquarters as the team prepped for their mission to the Nexus Point. Ethan was going to be accompanied by both Zin Xia and Sarah on this mission. Despite the potential danger, he was thrilled to go on this mission and explore the secrets of Nexus Point.

The Chronos Resurgence, pulsating with an ethereal glow, served as their sole gateway to the Nexus Point. Ethan, Zin Xia, and Sarah activated the devices with a resolute nod and a shared glance. A blinding flash engulfed them, followed by a disorienting space and time warp. In the blink of an eye, they were gone, leaving behind only the faint echo of their mission in the silence of the headquarters.

The Nexus Point was an amazing anomaly that defied comprehension on a human level. It was a nexus, a point of convergence where the past, present, and future intertwined rather than a location fixed in any particular era. Timelines combine to create a perplexing and breathtaking scene. Auroras in shades of green and violet blanketed the sky. The air itself crackled with an energy that defies explanation, a constant reminder of the fine balance that holds this strange world together.

It was a surreal experience for Ethan; he had never seen such a view in his entire life. They had to walk with extreme precautions, knowing that the ground beneath their feet could change to a different era with just one wrong step, creating an atmosphere of unnerving instability and breathtaking beauty.

Ethan noticed a brief glimpse of motion in the distance at that moment. There they were, the Temporal Renegades. With their figures dwarfed by the enormity of the swirling vortex of time, they stood brashly near the center of the Nexus.

"Alert! Team, there they are," said Ethan while firmly grasping his HEL Pistol.

"We have to cover them from every corner before they see us," said Sarah.

The Temporal Defense team encircled the unsuspecting Temporal Renegades from every direction with an obscure maneuver. Energy filled the air as HEL Pistols discharged their beams, the brilliant blue light cutting through the chaotic convergence of timelines.

Startled by the sudden assault, the Renegades retaliated, their energy weapons spitting fire. The Nexus Point echoed with the relentless hum of laser fire as the two sides clashed. One by one, the Renegades faltered, overwhelmed by the coordinated assault. Recognizing defeat, they beat a hasty retreat, their figures fading into the swirling vortex of time.

"That was a quick surrender," said Ethan.

"Something just doesn't add up," said Zin Xia with an alarmed expression. She continued: "What were they here for after all? What's exactly at the center of the Nexus Point?"

"There's only one way to find out," Ethan replied with a glint in his eye.

As the team got closer to the center of the Nexus Point, there was a tremor. A low hum reverberating through their bones seemed to emanate from the ground beneath their feet. A strange energy crackled in the air, sending chills down their spines.

Abruptly, an unseen force resembling a swirling kaleidoscope of temporal streams unfolded before them, swirling and merging in a mesmerizing dance pulsating with an otherworldly intensity that tore through them. All around them, dust and debris whirled into a frenzied state. Their hearts thumping their ribs, they instinctively braced themselves.

"Be careful, guys," said Sarah.

At that moment, a shadow materialized right in the center of the whirling vortex. It was not just a shadow but a void, an absolute absence of form and light. It writhed like a mass of pure darkness, pulsating and writhing. For an instant, this formless thing hovered in midair, a terrifying apparition beyond understanding. Then, it started to descend with purposeful slowness.

There was a chill shift as it got closer to the ground. The pitch-black darkness started to take on a solid form, changing and shaping strangely. It coiled and twisted, becoming something that looked like a human form, if hazy and covered in a disconcerting haze. The thing rose up, shadows swirling around it as if they were a shroud, hiding its features.

Then, a massive laugh echoed in the air from the figure, which sounded like multiple laughs mixed into one.

"What are you?" asked Ethan, his heart pounding out of his chest.

A voice boomed, resonating from everywhere and nowhere at once. It wasn't a human voice but a chilling chorus that scraped against their very souls.

"I am the Paradox," the entity continued, its formless visage solidifying further. "Created from a force of multiple paradox entanglements squeezing together from the many changes within time happening at the same time, you created me! Laughing; You with your misuse of the Chronos Resurgences. I am not a being but the embodiment of temporal dissonance itself. Time's corrupted echo. It is I who weave the strings of misfortune, manipulating the likes of the Temporal Renegades, the Temporal Conflux... even Temporal Weaver himself is but a pawn in my grand design."

"What do you want?' Ethan groaned.

"A singular purpose fuels my existence: to reshape the mere existence of time to my will. This universe, every planet within its grasp, shall be under my control. No longer will mere mortals dictate the flow of time. They will bow before me, their true master and their obedience will echo throughout eternity."

Despite the chill that emanated from the Paradox, Ethan stood tall, his voice unwavering. "You may be an embodiment of temporal dissonance," he declared, his gaze fixed upon the swirling entity, "but you underestimate the resilience of the human spirit. We are the Temporal Defense and will not stand idly by while you seek to play with the time. As long as Temporal Defense stands, we will be a thorn in your side, always ready to thwart your schemes."

He aimed his HEL Pistol at the entity and fired a laser beam, but it bounced off the Paradox and had no effect on him.

The paradox started eerily laughing with his distorted voice, and he said, "You silly human, you think you could stand a chance in front of me with your useless inventions. I am invincible."

With a flick of his hand, the Paradox unleashed a devastating shockwave that rippled through the Nexus Point. The Temporal Defense team, caught off guard by the sudden surge of temporal energy, was sent flying. They tumbled through the air, landing with heavy thuds upon the warped ground.

Getting back up from the ground, Zin Xia said: "Ethan, we can't fight him. We have no weapon that can even remotely challenge his power. We have to retreat."

Ethan felt a surge of defiance warring with the stark reality of the situation. "We can't just surrender and let him get away!" he yelled, his voice laced with a desperate intensity.

But a chilling realization dawned on them before he could say anything else. The Paradox, its form solidifying further, was levitating towards them with an unsettling slowness. Its dark, swirling eyes seemed to pierce through their very souls.

Chapter 16: Love's Resilience

The Paradox loomed closer, a monstrous anomaly crackling with raw malevolent energy. With each agonizing tremor, the ground beneath Ethan, Zin Xia, and Sarah threatened to crumble. He effortlessly hovered above the ground, with its cyclopean eye unblinkingly fixed on Ethan. Swinging his hand in a delicate way, he channeled the temporal energy of the Nexus Point from its surroundings.

Just when the Paradox was about to hit them with the next shockwave, Sarah whipped out the Chronos Resurgence and activated it. Just seconds before the wave was about to hit them, a blinding light erupted from the Chronos Resurgence, swallowing the whole team. The shockwave, deprived of its target, detonated in a deafening roar, carving a crater into the ground. In a blink, they were transported back to the safety of the Temporal Defense headquarters, leaving only the noise of devastation behind.

"That was too close for comfort!" said Sarah, catching her breath.

"Yeah, it was." Ethan groaned, rubbing a hand over his face, "I still can't believe we just... ran." The frustration was clear in his voice.

Zin Xia offered a calming presence. "Ethan," she said, her voice firm but gentle, "against the Paradox, without some kind of edge, it wouldn't have been a fight. It would have been a death wish."

"Yeah, Zin Xia is right!" said Sarah, her voice regaining some of its strength as she straightened her stance. "We may have retreated, but we're not done. Now we know what we're facing. We'll regroup, strategize, and next time, we'll be ready." She said, her eyes flashing with a newfound resolve.

Ethan's eyes lit with a glimmer of eagerness. He pushed himself off the wall and said, "Damn right. We will find a way to bring the Paradox down. However, first, we need to evaluate the damage and look for any signs of the temporal energy the Paradox was able to channel."

"Agreed. We also need to inform the head of Temporal Defense immediately. This is way bigger than just us now." Said Sarah.

Sarah hesitated for an instant before moving forward and giving Ethan a concerned look. "Ethan, are you okay though? Back then, you were hit pretty hard."

Ethan smiled a little. "Just a few bumps and bruises," he said, moving his arm and flinching a little. "There's nothing that a restful night's sleep can't solve."

Sarah looked at him for a second longer, then gave a curt nod. "All right," she said, a little softer in tone. "But try not to overwork yourself."

Ethan gently chuckled. "I wouldn't dream of it," he answered, "But hey, at least we can all agree to be prepared the next time."

Even though the Paradox won this time, the battle was far from over. Their near-death encounter had left them shaken, but it had also given them a newfound sense of purpose. They were just bruised and resolute, not broken. They were committed to completing their task, regardless of the consequences.

At night, when Ethan was alone in his room at the headquarters, there was a knock on the door. He swung the door open wider, surprised to see Zin Xia standing there. "Oh, hey, Zin Xia. Didn't expect you."

Her voice held a hint of concern. "Just wanted to check in and see how you're holding up after the Paradox encounter."

"Come in, come in," he ushered her inside.

Zin Xia cast a curious glance around the room. "Where are the rest of the agents who usually bunk here? Their beds seem awfully empty."

Ethan hesitated for a moment, his eyes darting away before meeting hers. "Oh, actually," he said, forcing a smile, "they're, uh, on a mission. So, I just have the place to myself for a while."

"That's nice!" she responded, sitting at the corner of the bed.

Ethan smiled again, looking at her.

Zin Xia's lips curved into a faint, wry smile. "You know, Ethan," she said, her voice soft, "you always manage to surprise me. Your bravery with the Paradox... was almost reckless, considering the power we were facing. Yet you were determined to defeat him. I have never seen that kind of courage before."

Ethan shifted uncomfortably, a flicker of self-consciousness crossing his features. "Maybe it was bravery, Zin Xia," he admitted, his voice low. "But... maybe there was something else too." He paused, running a hand through his hair. "Before Temporal Defense, before I stumbled upon the Chronos

Resurgence... life was just bland, you know? I never fit in anywhere and never really had friends. It felt like I was just drifting, existing but not really living, with no purpose."

He looked up at her, his eyes earnest. "Then I joined the Temporal Defense team. And suddenly, everything changed. It gave me a reason to get up every morning to push myself further. For the first time, I felt like I belonged somewhere, like I was a part of something big, and what I did actually mattered. Maybe I can't be some big hero everyone sees, like the ones in the history books. But the idea of being a silent guardian like you, someone who protects the timeline from the shadows... that's enough for me. It gives my life meaning."

Zin Xia's gaze lingered on Ethan a beat longer than necessary. "I'm glad I met you, Ethan," she said, her voice barely a whisper.

Ethan felt a warmth bloom in his chest. He returned her smile, a genuine one that crinkled the corners of his eyes. "I'm glad I met you too, Zin Xia."

The space between them seemed to shrink. Gaining confidence from the frankness in her gaze, Ethan extended his hand and delicately placed a loose hair behind her ear. Zin Xia felt the shock of his touch and made an unconscious move to lean into it. Their eyes locked, a silent conversation passing between them. Ethan felt his heart skip a beat.

At that moment, the weight of the Paradox, the fear of the mission, all faded away. The only sound that remained was Zin Xia's soft breath gently rising and falling against his ear, her body's warmth acting as a reassuring weight. Ethan closed his eyes, experiencing a calm energy. With Zin Xia at his side and in that quiet embrace, the world seemed a little less scary and a little more hopeful.

Ethan leaned back a smidge to look at Zin Xia's eyes again. Just then, she rushed in for a second kiss, a passionate one this time. Ethan kissed her back, holding her face with both of his gently, firm yet gently. He placed both his hands around her torso, embraced her tightly, and whispered in her ear, "Promise me that you will not disappear in the morning like last time."

Zin Xia placed her hand on the back of his head and whispered back, "I am not going anywhere. I will be right here next to you in the morning."

In the quiet aftermath of their kiss, a comfortable silence settled between them. Exhaustion tugged at their eyelids, the events of the day finally catching up. Ethan shifted closer, his arm wrapping instinctively around Zin Xia's waist. She nestled into his touch.

The night stretched before them. The mission, the Paradox, all of it seemed to fade into the background. All that remained was the gentle rise and fall of Zin Xia's breath against his ear, the warmth of her body a comforting weight against his. Ethan closed his eyes, a feeling of peace washing over him. In that quiet embrace, with Zin Xia by his side, the world felt a little less daunting, a little more hopeful. He fell asleep that night, a restful sleep fueled by the hope of a fresh dawn and the embers of desire.

A flash of auburn color appeared in Zin Xia's dark hair as the first ray of sunlight broke through the blinds. Ethan opened his eyes and felt a wave of relief upon realizing she was still there.

She slept soundly, a picture of tranquility. Her hair was gently splayed over the pillow. The tiniest hint of pink shaded her cheeks. In the quiet lull of sleep, she seemed different, unguarded. Ethan couldn't help but admire her.

Her eyes slowly opened, almost as if she could sense Ethan's gaze on her. She looked at him and gently smiled, "Good Morning."

"Morning, beautiful," Ethan responded.

"Did you sleep well?" she asked.

"Yes, I did, just like a baby."

A few days of rest offered a brief reprieve from the constant tension, but for Ethan and his team, preparation for the next encounter with the Paradox never truly stopped. Their training shifted from physical combat to an entirely new battlefield, which was learning how to manipulate temporal energy channeled from the Chronos Resurgence. Unlike any weapon they'd ever wielded, this power tapped into the very flow of time itself, granting them an arsenal with strange and devastating effects.

Attuning themselves to the Chronos' energy was similar to tuning a radio to a specific frequency, which required exposure to controlled temporal distortions to build resistance. Once attuned, the true potential of the Chronos unfolded. They could slow down enemies while remaining unaffected, essentially rewinding time to undo attacks or even teleport short distances through space and the flow of time itself.

Yet, wielding such power came with risks. Excessive use could lead to temporal sickness, and miscalculations could rip open unstable wounds in the timeline. The Paradox remained a mystery, his own manipulation of time an unknown factor. But as they delved deeper into the Chronos' secrets, Ethan and his team readied themselves for a clash against a master of temporal manipulation, a battle where victory could rewrite the story of history.

Two weeks of grueling training with Chronos energy left Ethan physically and mentally drained but far from unprepared. Their next mission was to mend the fractures and turbulences plaguing the timeline. But to do that, they had to travel back to The Nexus Point, the very same convergence where time flowed like a chaotic river. The danger was undeniable. Stepping into the Nexus Point was close to wading into a storm, the unpredictable energies swirling with the echoes of past, present, and future.

Yet, it was the only access point to mend the tears in time, the only way to prevent the fractures from unraveling history. The weight of responsibility pressed heavily on them. Success meant safeguarding the timeline. Failure... well, failure wasn't an option they dared contemplate. With a mix of apprehension and determination, Ethan and Zin Xia readied themselves for a perilous journey into the heart of the storm, a mission that could just as easily reunite them with their greatest nemesis, The Paradox.

In unison, Ethan and Zin Xia activated their Chronos Resurgence devices. A surge of temporal energy crackled around them, distorting the very air. With a blinding flash, they vanished from the confines of headquarters and reappeared amidst the chaotic storm of Nexus Point. The scene remained unchanged, a swirling inferno of temporal energy, remnants of past, present, and future churning together.

Wasting no time, Ethan and Zin Xia focused their Chronos energy from the Chronos Resurgence, channeling its power into mending the fractures that threatened to unravel the timeline. Just when they were almost finished mending the timelines of the past and the future, Ethan felt a pulsating force of power vibrate through him, a tangible presence, unlike the chaotic energy of the Nexus Point.

"What was that?" he said out loud.

"I'm not sure. It could be the temporal forces coming from the center of the Nexus point." Said Zin Xia.

"I don't think this is just that. It feels as if it had been deliberately produced..."

Before Ethan could finish, a distorted voice boomed through the swirling temporal chaos, a voice filled with chilling familiarity. "Fools, meddling where you don't belong!"

A surge of shockwave erupted from the voice's origin, a point deep within the Nexus Point's swirling energy. The force slammed into Ethan and Zin Xia, sending them flying through the chaotic currents. They tumbled through the temporal storm, their Chronos Resurgence devices flickering uselessly against the onslaught. As they hurtled towards the swirling depths of the Nexus Point, a single thought came into Ethan's mind: it was what they were exactly worried about, The Paradox.

Ethan groaned, pushing himself to his knees. His vision was blurry, the world tilting precariously around him. Beside him, Zin Xia mirrored his struggle, a snarl twisting her features.

Both of their Chronos Resurgence lay a few feet away, pulsating with a powerful glow that seemed to intensify with each passing second. Every fiber of Ethan's being screamed at him to reach it, but his body felt like lead.

"Zin Xia," he rasped, forcing the words past gritted teeth. "We need..."

She didn't wait for him to finish. She let out a helpless cry and dove for her Chronos Resurgence to seize it, her fingers grazing the cool metal as the floor gave way beneath them. Just then, they were sent sprawling by a second, more powerful shockwave. The wave caused Zin Xia to lose hold of her Chronos Resurgence again, and it began to roll dangerously toward the edge of the abyss that had opened from the force of temporal energy...

Chapter 17: The Paradox

Just seconds before Zin Xia's Chronos Resurgence was about to roll into the abyss, adrenaline jolted Ethan awake. Ignoring the throbbing pain in his limbs, he lunged for his Chronos Resurgence, which was lying a couple of feet away from him. The ground beneath started to crumble further, threatening to swallow them both. With a burst of desperate strength, he snatched the device and activated it. The temporal forces from his Chronos Resurgence caused the time to slow down for a few minutes in the Nexus Point. At that moment, Zin Xia sprinted towards her Chronos Resurgence and seized it before it fell into the abyss.

"That was a close call," said Ethan, wiping the sweat from his brow.

But the threat wasn't over. The monstrous voice of Paradox still echoed around the Nexus Point.

"We are not prepared for this," Zin Xia stated, her voice tight with controlled panic. "We should retreat. Two of us, even with the Chronos Resurgence devices, can't hope to stand against the Paradox."

Ethan locked eyes with her. "No, Zin Xia," he countered, his voice steady. "We can't leave again. Not this time. Not when so much is at stake. The past and the future hang in the balance. We can't abandon our mission. We have to fight."

A spark of admiration appeared in Zin Xia's eyes. "Are you sure about it, Ethan? This could cost us our lives, you know that, right?" she asked him.

"Yes, I am sure Zin Xia."

"Okay then, I'm staying too. There's no way I'm leaving you here alone with the Paradox." She responded, leaned into him, and kissed him on his lips. Ethan kissed her back.

A fiery spark of resolve burned in her eyes after the kiss. "All right, let's do this. But first, a plan. We can't just blindly charge in."

"Yeah, you're right. But we have to be quick; it will not be long until the temporal forces of Chronos Resurgence keep us protected," he replied.

"All right, so here's what I'm thinking," Zin Xia began. "The Paradox draws its power from the churning energy at the center of the Nexus Point. We need to split up. One of us creates a distraction for the Paradox, while the other makes a run for the center."

Ethan gestured towards their Chronos Resurgence devices. "Exactly. Whoever reaches the center can use their Chronos Resurgence to create a temporal shield around it. That should cut off Paradox's main source of energy, weakening him considerably."

A flicker of doubt crossed Zin Xia's face. "But creating a shield that big... it would drain the Chronos Resurgence completely. There's no way to know if it'll be enough to take him down."

"True," Ethan admitted, "but it's our only shot at evening the odds. We can worry about a permanent solution later. Right now, we need to buy some time." He met her gaze, his eyes filled with desperate hope.

"Who draws the distraction?" Zin Xia said as her lips formed a thin line. "The risk of getting close to the Paradox is higher. You should focus on the shield. I'm faster. I can create a better distraction."

Ethan shook his head. "No, you're the better strategist. We need you thinking clearly while I... well, while I cause some chaos."

A soft smile appeared on Zin Xia's lips. "Chaos is your specialty, isn't it?"

Ethan grinned, a spark of his usual bravery returning. "Exactly. Besides, I have a feeling the Paradox wouldn't appreciate a good old-fashioned bait-and-switch."

They knew the plan was risky, a desperate gamble against a seemingly invincible foe. But it was their only chance.

"All right," Zin Xia said with her voice resolute. "The Paradox's senses are likely attuned to the flow of temporal energy. We can use that to our advantage. When you create the distraction, you can focus on erratic bursts of energy, mimicking a potential breach in the timelines. It should draw his attention away from the center."

Ethan pointed towards the jagged rock jutting out from the ledge. "Use this as a springboard. It'll give you a momentary boost towards the center while I keep Paradox occupied."

Zin Xia nodded.

"Remember," Ethan said with his voice filled with concern, "the Chronos Resurgence can only handle so much temporal strain. You'll need to activate the shield as soon as you reach the core. Every second counts." Ethan squeezed her hand, a silent promise hanging between them. "I won't let you down, Zin Xia. We'll do this together."

Just like that, the temporal forces of Ethan's Chronos Resurgence that had slowed down the time minutes ago weakened, and the time went back to a normal pace. Following their plan, Zin Xia obscurely jolted towards the center of the Nexus Point while Ethan used the power of Chronos Resurgence to create a burst of temporal energy for luring in the Paradox.

At that moment, Ethan heard an echoing screech, which was likely a sign that the Paradox was now nearby. He prepared himself to confront the entity once again. As expected, the Paradox materialized seconds later, hovering menacingly towards Ethan from a distance. His hollow eyes locked onto Ethan. The space around him distorted due to the crackling temporal energy pulsating from him.

His distorted voice echoed with amusement. "So, the hero returns."

"You bet I am," Ethan replied. "And this time, I'm not leaving until you're finished,"

"That wouldn't be necessary. I can finish you with a snap of my finger in seconds." The Paradox mocked him.

"Is that right? Then try it." Ethan replied with an air of confidence.

"You're a feisty one, aren't you? And where did your friend go? Did she leave you here alone to face your fate?" the Paradox told him.

"I can defeat you on my own," Ethan grunted.

"You truly are delusional, ~~child~~. This fight is over before it even begins." He raised a hand, and a dark energy started crackling around his fingertips.

Just as the Paradox was about to unleash his attack, Ethan saw his chance. With a flick of his wrist, he channeled the power of his Chronos Resurgence once more. This time, however, the temporal energy didn't form a flashy burst. Instead, it wrapped around Ethan like a shimmering cloak, working as a shield to protect him from the shockwave the Paradox just released upon him.

The Paradox's laughter died in his throat, replaced by an expression of surprise. "What... what is this?"

Ethan grinned with a hint of recklessness in his eyes. "This, Paradox, is where things get interesting."

The Paradox snarled, his distorted voice booming. "I fear nothing! This trickery is meaningless! It is not going to last long."

Just as the Paradox lunged forward, a dark energy sphere crackled in his hand, and he aimed it again at Ethan. The temporal shield around Ethan was strong enough to protect him from the impact of the attack again.

Meanwhile, Zin Xia was sprinting towards the center of the Nexus Point. She could finally see it from a distance. As she finally approached the center, she pulled out her Chronos Resurgence. Activating the device, she used its temporal power to create a large temporal shield that covered the entire center of the Nexus Point, blocking the power supply for the Paradox. As she completed the shield, a tangible weakening occurred in the Nexus Point. The raw distortions in the surroundings started to disappear, and the air became calmer. Suddenly, a tremor shook the Nexus Point, shaking the ground beneath Zin Xia.

She braced herself, fearing the Paradox had somehow sensed her intervention. She was also worried about Ethan's safety while trying to distract the Paradox. Anything could happen. After a few seconds, the tremor stopped. Zin Xia hoped that it was just the raw temporal energy that often flowed through the Nexus Point.

At that time, Ethan huddled behind his diminishing temporal shield. His heart rate increased with each passing moment.

"Hurry up, Zin Xia," He faintly murmured. His shield was starting to weaken every second. Just then, the Paradox sent another powerful shockwave toward him that ended up breaking his temporal shield and exposing him directly to the danger in front of him.

"I told you, Nothing can stop me," The Paradox said with a disturbing cackle.

Ethan hurriedly tried to activate his Chronos Resurgence again, but he realized that it had lost its temporal powers. Now, it was just a normal artifact. Ethan desperately kept trying to activate it, even just for a few seconds. The Paradox started hovering closer to Ethan, slowly but menacingly.

"Come on!" Ethan yelled, holding his now powerless Chronos Resurgence.

"You are finished now!" the Paradox said in his distorting voice.

Just at that moment, a familiar voice came from behind him. "Not quite yet!" It was Zin Xia. Her arrival breathed hope into the dire situation. Upon hearing her voice, Ethan sighed in relief.

"Zin Xia, you made it," said Ethan.

"Yes, I did!" she responded with a smile.

With the Chronos Resurgence already in her hand, she activated it, and channeling its temporal powers, she blasted a powerful beam at The Paradox. The beam hit him directly, disrupting his balance. The Paradox raised his hand, trying to channel the temporal energy from the center of the Nexus Point, but this time, as he held his hand up, nothing happened. He tried to channel the energy again, now from its surroundings, but with the center now covered in the shield, the temporal forces around the Nexus Point had slowly dissipated, leaving him powerless.

"What did you do?" he yelled aggressively.

"We just cut your access to the center of Nexus Point, your main supply source of power," Zin Xia said with a smirk, "I guess now you are not as invincible as you said you were."

"That is not possible. I'll finish you too!" he screamed in anger and made another failed attempt to channel the temporal energy from his surroundings, but it was useless now.

The Paradox, who was once an imposing figure, now looked frail, with desperation twisting his features. Zin Xia held the Chronos Resurgence steady with another burst of temporal energy ready to launch at him.

Ethan stepped forward and said with his voice heavy with purpose, "This ends now. The innocent lives you've shattered, the timelines you've corrupted, they all weigh upon you."

The Paradox snarled, a pathetic imitation of his former power. "You can't erase everything I've done! Time is a river, ever-flowing, and my actions were a current within it!"

Ethan shook his head. "No, you were a dam, forcing the flow into unnatural directions. We are now finally guiding the river back to its course."

A resolute expression settled on Zin Xia's face. "With the Chronos Resurgence, we can undo the damage. But know this, Paradox, you are not erased. You shall exist within the Nexus Point, but only as a cautionary tale for those who dare tamper with the timeline again."

Raising the Chronos Resurgence high, Zin Xia aimed the pulsating light directly at the Paradox. A blinding white enveloped the entire place, momentarily drowning out all sound. When the light subsided, The Paradox was gone like smoke in the air. An eerie silence hung in the air, broken only by the ragged breaths of Ethan and Zin Xia.

Zin Xia lowered the Chronos Resurgence. A wave of exhaustion washed over both of their faces, the weight of the responsibility finally lifting.

Looking around the now-calm Nexus Point, Zin Xia said, "The fractures are mending. Timelines are realigning. The past cannot be changed, but the future... the future remains unwritten. We may not know what challenges lie ahead, but we face them together, with the knowledge of what almost was and the strength we've gained from this battle."

At that moment, a single tear traced its way down Ethan's cheek. "We did it, Xia. We saved our world, our timeline, countless others."

Zin Xia gave him a weak smile. "Together."

Ethan embraced her tightly. The battle was finally over. The air in the Nexus Point now crackled with a renewed energy, one that promised a future free from the distortions of The Paradox. The battle was finally won, not just with temporal powers but with courage and unity.

Chapter 18: A Journey Beyond Time

With the Paradox finally vanquished, the once-erratic flow of time in the Nexus Point had settled. All the distortions and fractures in the timelines have been amended. The temporal anomalies that had plagued the timestream, the rogue Temporal Renegades, the chaotic Temporal Confluxes, and the enigmatic Temporal Weaver all seemed to vanish along with their malevolent controller.

But their victory came at a cost; Ethan's Chronos Resurgence had lost its power. Yet, they were able to travel back to the headquarters from Nexus Point with the help of Zin Xia's Chronos Resurgence. Upon their arrival at Temporal Defense headquarters, they were greeted with a hero's welcome. Backslaps, congratulations, and relieved laughter echoed through the halls. Still, in the middle of the celebration, Ethan felt a sense of loss as he clenched his fist around the powerless device by his side.

This wasn't just a device but something that had accompanied Ethan throughout his journey through the temporal realms. He tried masking his sadness with a smile as he hugged Sarah. But she could tell something was off. Before Ethan could even think about telling her, Sarah asked, "You okay, rookie?"

"Yeah, I'm fine," Ethan mumbled, the smile faltering.

"Then why the long face?" she pressed gently.

Ethan hesitated, the words catching in his throat. Before he could muster a response, Sarah placed a hand on his arm, her touch grounding him. "It can't be nothing, Ethan. You know I can always tell."

His gaze dropped to the deactivated Chronos Resurgence in his palm. With a sigh, he pulled it out and showed it to Sarah.

"What about your Chronos Resurgence?" Sarah asked, trying to understand what had happened.

"It has lost its powers!" Zin Xia interjected.

Sarah gasped, her eyes flitting between the powerless device and Ethan's face. "Lost its power? How?"

"He used up all its temporal energy during the fight," Zin Xia explained.

Sarah felt sympathetic and squeezed Ethan's arm reassuringly. "Hey, it's okay. We'll figure out a way to restore it."

Ethan shook his head, and a flicker of despair appeared across his features. "I don't think it's possible."

Suddenly, a voice boomed from across the room, silencing the murmurs that had begun to rise. It was the director of Temporal Defense, Williams. His expression was uncharacteristically grim. "There might be a way," he declared, his gaze fixed on the deactivated Chronos Resurgence in Ethan's hand.

Ethan, Sarah, and Zin Xia all turned towards him, a spark of hope igniting in their eyes. "What is it?" Ethan asked.

"The Temporal Sage," Williams replied, his voice filled with reverence. "A legend whispered amongst our kind, an entity said to exist outside the flow of time itself, the one who imbued the Chronos Resurgence with their power."

A collective gasp rippled through the room. The Temporal Sage was a mythical figure, a being spoken of in hushed tones but rarely believed to be real.

"Seeking the Sage's aid is a perilous undertaking," Williams continued, his expression grim. "It requires not only a deed worthy of his attention but a journey beyond the charted territories of time. A place outside the reality we've ever known."

Ethan felt a chill of dread in his stomach. Although it was reassuring to think of a being who could restore the power of his Chronos Resurgence, the cost of asking for his help was intimidating. Was he really worthy of such help? Was he willing to take a chance on the unknown in order to have a second chance at reviving Chronos? Ethan thought.

"Where can we find Temporal Sage?" Ethan asked eagerly.

Director William's voice dropped to a hushed whisper. "The Temporal Sage is said to reside in the Chronos Gate, a hidden portal that is accessible only through specific temporal anomalies combined with the Chronos Resurgence." A place you have been before Ethan,

"What are the chances that he would be willing to help us revive Ethan's Chronos Resurgence?" asked Sarah.

"Ethan had helped mend the fracture in the timeline by defeating the Paradox. I believe Temporal Sage would at least be interested in hearing him for sure," Williams responded.

"It's worth a try, Ethan!" said Sarah with determination.

Ethan looked at Sarah and then at Zin Xia, "All right, we are going to Chronos gate." He exclaimed.

"Not so quick, rookie," Sarah added. "You need to get some rest, you and Zin Xia both."

"Well, now you've said it, I do feel tired." Said Ethan, stretching his arms with a smile.

Ethan got into his room to get some rest for the night. Lying on his bed, he waited for Zin Xia, hoping she would join him so they could have their moment in private. But after waiting for a while, she didn't come. He assumed she might have gone to sleep in her own room.

That night, Ethan was unable to sleep. Restless, he ventured out for a nighttime stroll. As he stepped outside for the walk, he spotted Zin Xia standing on the rooftop of the headquarters, gazing at the moon. Ethan, hoping to join her, went upstairs. She seemed almost otherworldly, with her hair flowing in the night breeze.

"Can't sleep?" he asked, his voice softer than usual.

She whirled around, startled, then a smile bloomed on her face. "Not really," she admitted. "What about you?"

"Yeah, same." He hesitated, then blurted, "What were you thinking about, Zin Xia?"

A sad expression appeared on her face. "Oh, nothing much. Just... how things will be once we reach Chronos Gate and revive your Chronos Resurgence."

Ethan leaned against the railing and felt a knot forming in his stomach. "What do you mean?"

"Well," she continued, glancing at the distance, "with the Paradox gone, there won't be many missions for the Temporal

Defense, will there? You'll... you'll probably have to go back home eventually."

The weight of her words settled heavily on him.

"Oh," he said, the realization hitting him like a punch. He hadn't thought that far ahead. Home. Leaving behind Sarah, the Temporal Defense... and Zin Xia. A storm of emotions churned inside him: fear, sadness, a desperate hope. He couldn't bear the thought of it all ending.

"It's strange, Zin Xia," Ethan admitted, a faint smile tugging at his lips. "Being here, fighting along your side, the Chronos Resurgence, the TDC with all its craziness, has actually started to feel like home."

She held his hand, her fingers crossing against his. "I know it has, Ethan. But what about your old life?"

A flurry of long-forgotten memories passed through his mind. He glimpsed himself again, not as a Temporal Agent, but as Ethan, Project Manager at one of Prime Meridian's leading tech firms. Evenings in Ethan's apartment used to be a mixture of routines and indulgence in his passion for relics. Then, his vision was filled with a glimpse of Temporal Defense headquarters. He was more than just the Project Manager here. Here, he was Agent Ethan, an essential part of a team.

The weight of accountability felt like a badge of honor rather than a burden. He felt a warm, genuine sense of belonging. For the first time, he mattered, not just to himself, but to something greater that cut through time. The difference was obvious and glaring. He was alive here. Back then, he was only existing.

"The truth is, Zin Xia," he confessed, his voice thick with emotion, "I've never felt this alive."

Zin Xia passed a faint smile.

"What about you, Zin Xia?" Ethan asked her. "What will you do"?

"I will probably go back to Ancient China, back to where I came from." Zin Xia responded.

"But why not stay here?" Ethan questioned curiously.

"I can't. My people need me back there." She paused for a moment to think and said, "You know, you could come with me too… if you decide to stay."

Ethan gasped. "I never thought about it." He exclaimed. It felt like a great opportunity, and he could explore the secrets of Ancient China further. But it meant leaving behind his old life back home. He was filled with mixed emotions. Although he knew he couldn't avoid these emotions forever, for now, to avoid feeling them, he chose to distract himself by changing the topic, "Well, if you have forgotten, we have a mission tomorrow. We have to travel to Chronos Gate to find Temporal Sage."

Zin Xia, sensing his turmoil, squeezed his hand gently, "Yes, you are right; we have a big mission tomorrow. We should try and get some sleep now." She replied.

Just like that, both Ethan and Zin Xia went downstairs to their designated rooms to sleep. The night felt longer than it usually did. Back in his room, Ethan was struck again by the thought of making the big decision. Finally, after a while of contemplating, his eyelids felt heavy, and he fell asleep.

The next morning, Ethan, Zin Xia, and Sarah geared up for their mission. Ethan clutched his powerless Chronos Resurgence, hoping for it to reactivate upon reaching Chronos Gate and meeting Temporal Sage. Zin Xia used her Chronos Resurgence for the mission; as she activated the device, the world around them shimmered, reality fracturing like a shattered mirror. When it solidified again, they stood in a place unlike any other: the Chronos Gate.

It wasn't a gate in the traditional sense but a swirling vortex of energy that defied explanation. Within the vortex, a sense of absolute stillness reigned. Here, the relentless flow of time ground to a halt, replaced by an eerie silence. It was as if they'd stepped into a frozen tableau, a snapshot of existence captured in a single, timeless moment. With a strange mixture of awe and nervousness, Ethan swallowed hard. This place was unlike any other place they had been before.

"Where do you think Temporal Sage will be?" Ethan asked his friends.

"Just hold on," said Zin Xia.

Just then, a low hum emerged from the swirling mass as if in response to her words. The slight tremor in the air began as a slight vibration and grew stronger with time. The vortex's ethereal mist started to swirl, growing faster and faster until it formed a blinding white core. Then, a loud crack reverberated through the eternal nothingness, and something started to take shape in the light.

It was an old man, his beard and hair as white as the light that surrounded him. On the other hand, his eyes were a striking contrast that looked like brilliant orbs that appeared to hold galaxies. His robes were tattered and had an otherworldly sheen to them, and every fold seemed to bear the weight of countless eons. The figure was towering over them, his intense gaze seeming to go right through their souls.

"Welcome, travelers," boomed a voice resonating through their bones. "You have come seeking the secrets of Chronos."

The Temporal Sage had arrived. His presence filled the air, radiating an ancient power that both terrified and exhilarated Ethan. This was it. The moment they'd been working towards.

"We are here because we need your help." Said Ethan in a shaky voice.

"And what makes you think you are worthy enough for my help?" Temporal Sage asked.

Ethan hesitated to answer. Zin Xia noticed his anxiousness and spoke for him, "He is the one who had defeated the Paradox and fixed all the distortions in the timeline."

Ethan spoke up, "Actually, I didn't do it on my own; she was with me," he pointed toward Zin Xia.

"Honesty. A rare and valuable trait these days. What's your name?" The Temporal Sage asked.

"My name is Ethan. I'm a temporal agent, and this is Zin Xia; she is a warrior." He answered.

"Fascinating." he paused for a moment. "Ethan," the Temporal Sage spoke, his words weaving through the currents like a gentle breeze, "your choices have guided the course of history, and the threads of time have converged upon the nexus point. The ambitions of Paradox have been thwarted, and the timeline has been restored to its intended path."

Ethan's gaze remained steady as he regarded the Temporal Sage. "The power of unity and the resilience of love have proven to be the greatest forces against any manipulation," he responded, his voice carrying a quiet resolve, "and it is through those forces that we have preserved the integrity of time."

The Temporal Sage's presence seemed to shimmer with approval, his gaze reflecting a sense of satisfaction. "You have proven yourself to be a guardian of time, a protector of the threads that weave the fabric of reality," He said, "and your journey has left an indelible mark on the tapestry of existence."

Ethan felt a sense of pride. He had faced challenges that transcended the boundaries of time, and through his journey, he had come to understand the intricacies of existence itself.

"So, tell me, what help do you need from me? It would be my honor." The Temporal Sage asked.

"My Chronos Resurgence lost its power when we defeated the Paradox. I have been told that if anyone can help restore its powers, it's you." Ethan told him, holding out his Chronos Resurgence

"You've come to the right place for that." The Chronos Resurgence in Ethan's hand pulsed once, then twice. A warm light emanated from it, growing brighter with each beat. The lifeless metal seemed to have reawaken. It rose slowly, hovering in the air like a reborn star. Then, with a soft chime, it settled back into Ethan's palm, no longer inert but humming with a potent energy.

"Many people believe that it's them who find the Chronos Resurgence when, in fact, it's the other way around. The Chronos Resurgence chooses its own master. Ethan, it was destined for you to find it." Temporal Sage told him with a gentle smile.

Ethan gasped in fascination, holding his revived Chronos Resurgence. It was all meant for him in his destiny, this whole journey through the tapestry of time.

He questioned, "So if finding the Chronos Resurgence was in my destiny, with time restored now, what will be my destiny now? Will it still be in the future or back home to my normal life?"

The Temporal Sage gazed at Ethan, "It all depends on your choice, a choice that would shape your destiny. I believe you will follow your heart and make the right decision." His voice conveyed a gentle understanding, as if he could read the thoughts that filled Ethan's mind.

The complexities of the decision weighed heavily on him, a decision that held the power to reshape the course of his life. He could stay in his own time, which held familiarity with the world he had known. But in his heart, a different path beckoned, leading him to a life entwined with Zin Xia's in the past. Their connection had defied the constraints of time, their bond forged through shared experiences and shared challenges. He knew that his choice would shape not only his fate but the fate of the woman he loved...

Chapter 19: Building a Legacy

As Ethan grappled with his indecision, his gaze drifted to Zin Xia, stirring a complex blend of emotions within him. With a heart heavy with longing and determination, he closed his eyes briefly, allowing memories to flood his mind. Ethan relived every moment in his mind's eye, from the very first time he heard about her to their first meeting and everything they had done together. He understood that his and her hearts were inextricably linked by love, a bond that had withstood uncertainty and temporal manipulation.

With a bittersweet smile and newfound resolve, Ethan experienced a moment of clarity. He turned to the Temporal Sage, his voice firm. "For years, I've searched for the true purpose of my life," he began. "But when I met Zin Xia, it reignited the flame within me. Fate had brought me here, and I've discovered a new chapter I'm ready to write."

He turned towards Zin Xia, his gaze locked with hers, and continued, "Zin Xia," he croaked, his voice raw with emotion. "You asked me about coming to Ancient China with you, and after all this time thinking, all I can see is... us. There. Together. The answer is yes. I want to come with you."

Zin Xia's eyes turned teary, filled with emotions as she met Ethan's gaze. "Our connection transcends time itself," she said, her words a reflection of their shared journey, "and I welcome this new chapter with an open heart."

The Temporal Sage's presence seemed to radiate with approval as if time itself resonated with Ethan's and Zin Xia's choice. "The strings of existence are constantly reshaped by the choices of those who navigate its currents," he told them with a gentle smile.

Ethan went for Zin Xia's hand and grabbed it; his fingers intertwined, and they stood together. They had a shared understanding and looked at each other with an unspoken understanding. Zin Xia squeezed his hand, the warmth a grounding force amidst the storm of emotions. They looked back into each other's eyes and knew that they were about to start a new chapter of life and that regardless of how things would be, they would be together.

With her heart brimming with warmth, Sarah saw their connection and smiled. It was a future brimming with possibilities, and she couldn't help but be happy for them. Just like that, not only was Ethan's Chronos Resurgence powers restored, but he also made a big decision.

With a final look of gratitude towards the Temporal Sage, Ethan and Zin Xia bowed deeply. Ethan used the new powers of his Chronos Resurgence to help them travel back to TDC headquarters.

A few days drifted by at the bustling TDC headquarters. Unlike their usual whirlwind of temporal missions and assignments, these days were a welcome reprieve. Ethan and Zin Xia spent their last days with Sarah and the familiar crew. As their departure came near, the crew threw them a farewell party.

Finally, the last day arrived at TDC headquarters before Ethan and Zin Xia embarked on their journey to Ancient China. A bittersweet melancholy had settled over them and also the crew.

Ethan packed up all his things in his bag, including his clothes, some artifacts he had collected as souvenirs from different missions they had been to, his HEL Pistol, and his Chronos Resurgence. He met every member of the crew to say his goodbyes. The air crackled with unspoken emotions as Ethan approached Sarah. A silence hung between them, a stark contrast to their usual banter.

Sarah, her eyes teary despite a playful smile, gripped his shoulders. "Rookie," she said, her voice thick with emotion, "you've come a long way since those first fumbling days with the Chronos Resurgence."

Ethan scoffed; a hint of his old self peeking through. "Come on, Sarah, even you have to admit I'm not a rookie anymore."

She winked, a mischievous glint in her eyes. "Perhaps not to everyone. But you'll always be my rookie." Her playful jab softened into a warm embrace. "You'll do great things out there, Ethan. I never doubted you for a second."

Ethan squeezed her back, the weight of her words settling in. "Thanks, Sarah. What about you? What are you planning to do?"

"This place," Sarah gestured around the bustling headquarters, her voice filled with quiet pride, "will always be my home. I will be staying here. And you, Ethan, are always welcome back. No mission is too big, no timeline too altered that we wouldn't open our doors to you."

A smile, genuine and heartfelt, spread across Ethan's face. "I definitely will," he promised. The weight of their future pressed down on him, a thrilling mix of uncertainty and anticipation. He was leaving behind a family he'd never known he needed, but the time had come to write his own chapter, one filled with adventure and purpose, alongside Zin Xia.

As Ethan and Zin Xia, all packed up, started to activate their Chronos Resurgence for their travel, Ethan's gaze swept across the room, taking in the familiar faces. This very environment had become a second home. A pang of sadness settled in his chest as reality sunk in: this was goodbye.

"Goodbye, you guys. I'm gonna be missing each of you!" he announced with teary eyes as the light emanated from the Chronos Resurgence.

"We'll miss you too!" said Sarah with a smile.

Just like that, the bright light from the Chronos Resurgence engulfed Ethan and Zin Xia, and they vanished into thin air.

On the other side, they materialized at the Great Wall of Ancient China. The Great Wall snaked across the rugged landscape; the air was clean and crisp with a hint of earthy and woodsmoke scent. Ethan inhaled deeply as the sight of the ancient past tickled his skin, his senses overwhelmed by the visual feast. This was ancient China, just like he remembers from his first visit—a thrill shot through him, a desire to discover the mysteries this ancient time preserved.

Zin Xia, noticing his excitement, added, "So, are you ready for the new chapter?"

"Yes, I've never been more ready, Zin Xia!" he told her, locking his gaze on her and grasping her hand.

A figure emerged from the shadows at the foot of the wall, his conical hat casting a long shadow over his face. He carried a wooden stick with him to help him walk. As he came closer, Ethan recognized the man; it was Lei Wei, the guide who had aided them on their previous mission to ancient China. A warm smile creased his weathered face as he recognized them. His greeting, though simple, held a wealth of unspoken understanding.

"Welcome back," Lei Wei said, his voice raspy but kind.

With the weight of the journey momentarily forgotten, Ethan responded with a genuine grin. "Lei Wei, it's good to see you again."

"Hello, both of you. I've been waiting for your arrival." He told them.

"You've known that we were coming?" Ethan asked curiously.

"Yes, sir. I've known you'd be back one day with our warrior Zin Xia." He smiled. "Now, come along!"

Ethan and Zin Xia trailed behind Lei Wei, their eyes flitting over the amazing scene. The altitude of the crisp, thin air carried the distant clang of unseen activity. The old stones beneath their feet felt like they were carrying the weight of the past as they walked over them.

Their journey continued for what seemed like hours, with only the occasional bird chirp or the rustle of leaves in the arid wind to break up the monotony of their footsteps. Ethan's legs grew tired with the long walk, but he was more occupied with his curiosity. With each turn came a new view, including a watchtower in disrepair, a weathered signpost with faded characters etched on it, and a lone warrior silhouetted against the distance.

Finally, Lei Wei stopped in front of a magnificent building that rose out of the ground like a phoenix from the ashes. It was an ancient Chinese temple with centuries of experience infused into its fabric. The elaborately patterned facade was a classic example of traditional architecture. Shining, glazed tiles, carefully arranged in vivid red and gold, glinted in the afternoon sun, bathing the surroundings in a warm orange light.

The roofline was decorated with carved representations of legendary animals, such as phoenixes with spread wings and dragons with sinuous coils, whose watchful eyes appeared to follow their every move. A subtle buzz of old rituals and unspoken prayers surrounded the temple.

"This is breathtaking!" Ethan gasped.

"This is barely just the beginning of it," Zin Xia smirked at him.

You will be staying here, at the Temple of the Jade Emperor," Lei Wei announced.

Ethan, Zin Xia, and Lei Wei stepped through the Temple of the Jade Emperor's threshold, and the carved guardians on the roofline appeared to be holding their breath. The air inside was cool and surprisingly still, a welcome contrast to the heat that had shimmered off the ancient stones outside. The air carried a light incense smell and the faint smell of old wood and paper.

The interior was large and open, with a high ceiling held up by enormous, richly carved pillars. Draped from the rafters were banners of deep crimson silk, intricately embroidered with gold thread dragons. There was a palpable sense of history pressing down on Ethan's shoulders as the air hummed with a quiet reverence.

Lei Wei pointed to a cluster of robed figures at the far end of the hall tending to an elaborately decorated altar. The monks bowed their heads in greeting.

Lei Wei said in a low voice, "These are the Guardians of the Temple. They were anticipating your arrival."

Ethan was truly fascinated by everything. The days that followed at the Jade Emperor's Temple were filled with intense training and revelation. Once an intimidating presence, the Guardians now served as their patient teachers. Ethan met Master Zhao, an elderly, wise monk with a depth of knowledge that went beyond scripture. He described the past, present, and future as being interconnected, comparing time to a constantly flowing river where changes in one area could have unanticipated effects on another.

Before the sun rose, Ethan would meditate. He would breathe in the clean mountain air and watch the sky turn orange and gold as the sun rose. Master Zhao taught him how to focus his thoughts and access his inner energy as he led him through traditional breathing exercises. This renewed emphasis permeated his physical training.

He learned martial arts from the stoic monk with the katana, who was only addressed as Master Ken. Master Ken moved with a deadly grace that blended power and accuracy; poetry was in motion. Beneath the guarding gaze of the dragon and phoenix sculptures that graced the temple courtyard, Ethan acquired the skill of Wushu, whereby his body transformed into an extension of his will.

His initial awkwardness soon gave way to a newfound fluidity. The temple monks taught him the fighting techniques and the underlying philosophy. It wasn't just about overpowering an opponent but about understanding the flow of energy and a fight's ebb and flow.

Ethan adapted seamlessly to the training. His movements were swift and precise, his dagger flashing like a deadly silver streak in the morning sun. She sparred with Ethan often, their initial clanging clashes soon evolving into a dance of feints and parries. Zin Xia, who was already equipped with this art, would watch Ethan training and motivate him to push further.

A friendship developed between Ethan and the people of the temple. Master Wei would unfurl ancient scrolls, their delicate rice paper filled with cryptic symbols and faded ink. Under the flickering candlelight, he would unravel stories of forgotten heroes and temporal anomalies long since rectified. Ethan learned of powerful artifacts hidden across time, past paradoxes threatening reality and of the Temporal Guardians, a silent order dedicated to safeguarding the flow of time.

With each passing day, Ethan felt a shift within himself. The brash Temporal Agent slowly gave way to a more centered, focused individual. He craved not just the thrill of action but the underlying understanding of his role in the grand scheme of things. The Temple of the Jade Emperor, with its serene beauty and ancient wisdom, was becoming a sanctuary, a place where he could hone his skills and prepare for the challenges that lay ahead.

One evening, Ethan and Zin Xia went to a hilltop to watch the sunrise. Atop the windswept peak, the world unfolded beneath them. Dawn was a slow, majestic unfurling, painting the eastern sky in hues of rose and gold. Ethan and Zin Xia sat shoulder-to-shoulder, a comfortable silence settling between them. He watched the first rays of sunlight kiss the temple rooftops below, igniting a spark of gratitude.

"Zin Xia," he began, his voice low and thoughtful. "I never thought my life would take this turn. Waking up to breathtaking sunrises like this, learning from the temple monks… it feels right. Like a missing piece has finally clicked into place."

Zin Xia met his gaze, a gentle smile gracing her lips. "I'm glad you came too, Ethan. This journey has been… unexpected, to say the least."

A contemplative silence fell between them once more, broken only by the soft sigh of the wind. Ethan's mind wandered, picturing their future after this mission. The rigorous training, companionship with the temple monks, and a sense of purpose that resonated within the ancient temple walls all felt strangely familiar. He had an epiphany.

"What if," he mused aloud, a sudden thought striking him, "we built a branch of the Temporal Defense Corporation here in Ancient China? We could call it the Timekeepers." Ethan told her.

Zin Xia's smile widened, an intriguing glint in her eyes. "Ethan," she began, a hint of amusement laced in her voice, "what I'm about to tell you might sound crazy."

Ethan's brow furrowed. "Crazy? Hit me."

"Well," she continued, her voice dropping to a whisper, I've seen glimpses of this story unfold long before you ever stepped into it. I knew the truth, but I couldn't say anything. Time is a delicate fabric, and events have to unfold at their own pace."

Ethan curiously listened.

Leaning closer, her gaze held a profound intensity. "Ethan, you didn't stumble upon the Temporal Defense Corporation. You found it. Here, in Ancient China. This is where it all begins." She confessed.

Ethan's jaw dropped. "Me? But... the TDC found me." Disbelief warred with a dawning sense of wonder.

Zin Xia chuckled softly. "Time is a funny thing, Ethan. It doesn't always flow in a straight line. It works in unfathomable ways. You have a long, extraordinary journey ahead of you. One where you'll lead countless Temporal Agents, protecting the delicate balance of time itself."

The weight of this revelation settled on Ethan's shoulders. He, the brash rookie, a normal guy, was destined for something far grander. He looked at Zin Xia, then back at the horizon, the rising sun painting the sky in hopeful gold. A new sense of purpose bloomed within him, a responsibility not just to the present but to the very fabric of time itself. He was no longer just Ethan, a Temporal Agent. He was going to be the founder and the leader of the timekeepers. And his journey, it seemed, was only just beginning.

Chapter 20: Eternity's Embrace

Three years had melted away like sand through an hourglass, leaving behind a legacy far grander than Ethan could have ever imagined. Amidst the timeless beauty of Ancient China, he found the headquarters of the Timekeepers, a place built to protect the flow of time. It was a paradox, a tangled loop of time that had initially defied comprehension. He would still wonder how he could have founded the organization that trained him to mend the fabric of time itself. But then, Zin Xia's words would echo in his mind: time doesn't always flow in a straight line. This, it seemed, was his predestined path, a circle of time elegantly completed.

Slowly, the pieces clicked into place. The Chronos Resurgence, the device that once used to be a chance discovery, has now revealed its true purpose. It was the key, the catalyst that unlocked his destiny. He was chosen not just to become a Temporal Agent but to be the very foundation upon which the Temporal Defense Corporation would be built. Ethan, the once-ordinary project manager, had become the architect of a legacy. He and Zin Xia, the pioneers, stood at the precipice of time, guardians against those who would disrupt the delicate balance of the past, present, and future.

The creation of the Timekeepers wasn't a sudden event but a gradual, organic process. It all began with the wisdom gleaned from the temple monks. Master Wei unraveled the philosophy of the secrets of time travel, how to navigate the ever-shifting currents of history, identify and repair temporal anomalies, and blend seamlessly into any era without disrupting the delicate balance. Beyond theory, Ethan and Zin Xia drew upon their own experiences to craft a practical curriculum. Master Ken, a stoic figure with a katana glinting at his hip, instilled in him the deadly grace of Wushu, transforming Ethan into a focused warrior. So, he was finally fully ready to lead the Timekeepers.

But the Timekeepers weren't just about strength and knowledge. They needed the right people, individuals with hearts of steel and minds sharp as honed blades. Ethan and Zin Xia, drawing from their travels across different eras, handpicked potential agents. They searched for a specific blend, including a thirst for adventure, a rock-solid moral compass, and the mental fortitude to navigate the paradoxes of time. These recruits weren't just soldiers; they were the future of Timekeepers. Ethan saw the potential in each of them, the raw talent waiting to be nurtured.

Ethan and Zin Xia poured their knowledge and experience into these fledgling agents, preparing them for the challenges that lay ahead. These first years were a whirlwind of construction, training, and recruitment. The grand halls of the Jade Emperor Temple became the Timekeepers' first headquarters, a place where the weight of the past intertwined with the promise of the future. As the years rolled by, the Timekeepers grew, each new recruit adding a piece to the intricate puzzle Ethan had set in motion. It was a legacy built on a paradox, a circle of time elegantly completed.

One evening, the wind whipped around Ethan and Zin Xia as they stood on the rooftop of the Timekeepers' headquarters, gazing out over the sprawling complex established amidst the ancient Chinese landscape. Three years. It felt like both a lifetime and a blink of an eye.

Ethan turned to Zin Xia, a wry smile playing on his lips. "We did it, Zin Xia. This is it. The Timekeepers. Looking back, it feels like every victory, every setback, every near-death experience… it all led to this moment. One different decision, one wrong turn, and things could have been so different."

Zin Xia met his gaze, her eyes sparkling with a knowing warmth. "Not necessarily, Ethan," she said gently. "I believe our fate always finds its way to us. The events that were meant to find us always find a way, no matter the twists and turns we take along the path."

Ethan considered her words, a sense of wonder washing over him. Perhaps she was right. The very fabric of time, with its paradoxes and non-linearity, had brought them here. He, a man pulled from his ordinary life, and Zin Xia, a guardian sworn to protect the flow of time, their paths had intertwined, destined to create this very place that will be protecting the timeline for the rest of eternity.

He squeezed her hand, "So, what's next?" he asked, a thrill of anticipation coursing through him. "Do we have our first temporal anomaly to tackle?"

Zin Xia's smile widened. "There's always an anomaly, Ethan. But for now," she said, leaning into him, "let's just savor this moment. We built something extraordinary here. A legacy." Ethan wrapped his arm around her, the weight of their accomplishment settling comfortably on his shoulders.

As more years passed and the Timekeepers flourished, Ethan and Zin Xia found themselves in the twilight of their careers with the organization. Their bond had blossomed into a family, with children who were raised amidst the unique responsibilities of safeguarding the flow of time.

Ethan, now weathered by experience and tempered by wisdom, knew it was time to entrust the responsibility of leading the Timekeepers to the capable hands of the next generation of agents who had proven themselves worthy. However, before Ethan could retire, Zin Xia revealed to him a final, cryptic mission that would tie together the ends of his life's timeline and bring closure to his journey.

"What is it, Zin Xia?" Ethan inquired, his curiosity piqued by her mysterious revelation.

"We must journey back to 2036, to Prime Meridian," Zin Xia informed him. "This will be your last mission, Ethan. It is the most crucial one as it will tie together all the threads of your journey."

"Prime Meridian? My old home before I joined TDC?" Ethan's mind raced with memories and questions. "But why?"

"You will find out in due time," Zin Xia replied with a gentle smile.

Trusting implicitly in her guidance, Ethan and Zin Xia activated their Chronos Resurgence, the device that had been their faithful companion through countless temporal adventures, and set off on their final mission. They materialized outside an abandoned research facility in Prime Meridian in the year 2036.

"This place..." Ethan began, his voice trailing off as he took in the familiar surroundings.

"You recognize it, don't you?" Zin Xia said, her tone filled with knowing.

Ethan nodded slowly, the pieces of the puzzle falling into place. "This is where it all began. Where I found my Chronos Resurgence."

"Yes, Ethan. This is where your journey truly began," Zin Xia confirmed, her eyes sparkling with ancient wisdom.

"But why are we here now?" Ethan questioned, a mixture of anticipation and apprehension building within him.

"We are here to complete the circle, to ensure that your past self follows the path that has led you here," Zin Xia explained cryptically. "It is time to close this chapter of your life, Ethan, and embrace what lies ahead."

As they made their way inside the facility, Ethan's heartbeat was a mixture of nostalgia and anxiousness. They came inside to the old control room, the place where Ethan had first laid eyes on the Chronos Resurgence and felt the stirrings of destiny. With a sense of reverence, Ethan approached the spot where the device had once rested, his hands trembling slightly as he prepared to return it to its rightful place in the timeline.

"But didn't I find the Chronos Resurgence? Why do I have to put it back?" Ethan questioned, his mind grappling with the paradoxical nature of their mission.

"Ethan, it is a paradox," Zin Xia explained patiently. "By returning the device to its original location, you ensure that your past self discovers it and embarks on the journey that has led you to this moment. It is the closing of a loop, the fulfillment of a destiny that spans across time."

Reluctantly, Ethan placed the Chronos Resurgence back where it belonged, feeling a bittersweet pang as he let go of the device that had been his constant companion throughout his journey.

"It will find me," Ethan whispered, a quiet reassurance to himself as he stepped back from the control panel.

Zin Xia smiled warmly, her eyes reflecting the depth of their shared experiences and the bond forged through countless trials and tribulations. Suddenly, they heard footsteps approaching the control room.

"Someone's coming in," Ethan whispered.

Quickly, they rushed to hide behind a wall. Ethan quietly peeked through the little space on the corner and watched his younger self enter the room. He saw the wonder and excitement in his past self's eyes as he discovered the Chronos Resurgence for the first time, grasping the Chronos Resurgence in his hand for the setting in motion the chain of events that would ultimately lead him to become the man he was today. He finally felt a sense of closure wash over him. He knew that his journey might be ending here, but for his past self, it was only the beginning.

With the mission accomplished and the circle of time closed, Zin Xia activated her Chronos Resurgence one final time and journeyed back to Ancient China. Ethan finally retired with a sense of peace and fulfillment. He devoted himself to spending more time with Zin Xia and their children, savoring the tranquility of their lives in Ancient China. In the midst of the lush landscapes and timeless beauty of their surroundings, Ethan and Zin Xia found solace and contentment. They watched with pride as their children grew and flourished, each one carving out their own unique path in life.

As the years passed, Ethan and Zin Xia cherished the simple joys of everyday life, relishing each moment spent together as a family. They shared laughter and stories, passing down the wisdom gleaned from their adventures as Timekeepers to the next generation. Though their days of traversing time were behind them, Ethan and Zin Xia found comfort in the knowledge that their legacy would endure. They knew that the bonds they had forged and the memories they had created would transcend the passage of time, leaving an indelible mark on the world.

As Ethan reflected on his journey with gratitude and fondness, he found peace in the realization that they had made a difference, not only in preserving the fabric of time but also in shaping the lives of those they loved. And as he looked to the future with hope and optimism, he knew that their legacy would live on for generations to come.

Epilogue: Threads of Eternity

Years had passed since Ethan and Zin Xia's final mission, and their legacy as the Guardian of time had been engraved on the walls of the caves of Ancient China. *TimeKeepers*, the organization they had built, had grown and flourished, expanding its reach across the ages and safeguarding the flow of time for generations to come. In the halls of the Timekeepers' headquarters, portraits of Ethan and Zin Xia were hung on the walls, reminding them of the extraordinary journey that had led to the creation of their timeless legacy. Their story inspired countless agents who followed in their footsteps, each carrying forward the torch of their mission with pride and determination.

Decades morphed into centuries, and the TimeKeepers, the organization they birthed, had blossomed into a formidable force later expanded by Temporal Defense Corporation (TDC). As for Ethan and Zin Xia themselves, they had found peace and fulfillment in their retirement, content to spend their days together in the tranquil beauty of Ancient China. The Temporal Defense Corporation missions had only started.

Now and then, rumors of temporal anomalies would catch their attention, igniting a flashback of their former spirit of adventure. Maybe it was an artifact unearthed from a far-off past, a ripple in the stream of time, or a mysterious message from an unknown era. For Ethan, it would be like placing a piece of a puzzle into its place that he had already solved before. Every unfolding event started to connect beautifully, painting the full picture of his entire journey through time or what his past self had yet to experience.

There would be days when their former friends from TDC, including Sarah and other team members, would visit them in Ancient China. Sarah, her hair now streaked with silver, would recount the latest missions, her eyes twinkling with the same youthful spirit. Other teammates, their faces stamped with the passage of time, shared stories and laughter, rekindling the companionship of their collective past.

Within the warmth of these reunions, Ethan sometimes felt a pang of longing. A yearning to revisit his younger self, to relive the thrill of those early missions, the thrill of his rookie days. He'd imagine himself back in the busy halls of the Temporal Defense Corporation headquarters, the weight of responsibility yet to settle on his shoulders. But then, a familiar warmth would brush against his hand, grounding him in the present. Zin Xia, her gaze filled with understanding, would offer a gentle nudge.

"There's another Ethan out there, isn't there?" she'd say, "Just starting his journey, filled with the same nervousness and excitement you once felt."

His past—with all of its struggles and victories—was an important part of the fabric of history. It had molded him into the man he was now, standing by Zin Xia as a rock of stability for their bond. The unwritten Path, the thought of alternate choices, of roads not taken, would occasionally cloud his mind. "What if?" he'd wonder, picturing a different life path. But Zin Xia would bring him back.

"Fate," she would say, "has a way of weaving its magic. The choices we make, big or small, shape our path, but the destination... the destination is often predetermined."

Ethan wouldn't necessarily agree, but he found solace in her words. The past was an immutable force, a stepping stone on the path they were meant to walk. The future, however, remained a vast, uncharted territory brimming with possibilities. Zin Xia had carefully hidden the Chronos Resurgence in a hidden compartment of their home. They didn't make this decision hastily. They'd had countless conversations leading them here, full of the bittersweet nostalgia of their past together.

What was once a symbol of their exciting temporal adventures, the Chronos Resurgence, now was a powerful anchor to reaffirm their commitment to one another to live in the moment and let time pass organically. As Ethan looked into Zin Xia's eyes, a lifetime of joint experiences reflected there, he knew that whatever challenges awaited, they would face them together.

Surrounded by their children and grandchildren, they reveled in the simple joys of family life, cherishing each moment spent together as a precious gift. Though their days of traversing time were behind them, Ethan and Zin Xia's bond remained as strong as ever, parading the enduring power of love and companionship. And as they looked out over the landscape of their lives, they knew that their journey had been worth every moment.

For, in the end, they had not only preserved the fabric of time but also forged a legacy that would endure for eternity— a legacy built on courage, sacrifice, and the unbreakable bonds of friendship. And as they watched the sun set on another day, they knew that their story was far from over, for the adventure of a lifetime was always just around the corner.